Paperback ISBN Number: 978-1-9991550-0-1

Book Design by Claire Whitmore

author.clairewhitmore@gmail.com
Clairewhitmore.weebly.com

To my children,
May you always follow the path your heart leads you down.
Your head may try to deter you,
But your heart will never fail to ensure your life is filled with magic.

Thank you both for the endless love and support.
It is because of you both that I have had the courage to break the mould and follow my dreams.

Life never really ends up as you planned. Sure, there are moments that resemble the general idea, paths walked that felt like you were following your dreams and your own set of rules, but the funny thing about all of it, is that we simply can't predict when, or who, will walk into our line of sight that can throw everything off balance, that can undeniably alter our worlds, no matter how hard we try to stay focused on our end goal. Sometimes, what we thought was a settled and happy life, simply isn't enough. Sometimes we need to trust our souls when they are screaming at us to open our eyes and hearts and leap off the safe path because, at the end of it all, you just might find that earth-shattering happiness that only the lucky few ever get to experience.

Out Of Nowhere

One

First Impressions

Hailey Nelson had met Will Jenkins eight years ago through work. It was not love at first sight, nor was it a romance that anyone saw coming, including Hailey or Will. Will was married at the time and nearly ten years older than she was. Although mature for her age, Hailey was wildly inexperienced with relationships and never saw herself as the girl guys had much interest in as far as dating went. She considered herself sort of a plain Jane type, although that spoke more to her self confidence than how the world actually saw her. She kept her brown hair long and since it had its own natural wave to it, she never felt she needed to do much to it. She was never the girly type of girl and growing up, most of her childhood friends had been boys. Because of that, she naively assumed that that's how most men saw her and since she was fairly shy, she was always afraid she didn't know how to really approach guys or allow them to truly see her. The thing she didn't realize was, that more often than not, when she walked into a room, everyone noticed. She was always just too busy focusing on how uncomfortable and nervous she was to see it.

Will was not a game player and didn't like the way things were going at the advertising company they worked for. In a business dedicated to creativity and thinking outside the box, he found their office stuck in a rut and thought things should be focused on reality and letting the actual art speak for itself, not creating something to be portrayed in a way to get false or over dramatized attention. It set his mood even before walking through the door, let alone into a meeting. Which was where he and Hailey had their first opportunity to meet.

She was seated at the table, eager to be professional at twenty-one years old, fresh out of college and feeling like she had the world at her feet. In walked Will, among the others who were taking part in the meeting. He chose to sit at the end of the table, almost as if to ensure some form of authority when he inevitably felt the need to shoot down ideas. His chair turned a touch to the side, giving the impression that he just might get up and leave if things weren't going the way he liked. One foot out the door so to speak.   Throughout the meeting, he stared at his pen, tapping it lightly on the pad of paper in front of him. Never so much as making eye contact with anyone. Luckily for him, this meeting was more of an introduction of the newest members of the team, Hailey being one of them; than an overview of the latest projects that were in development, so there wasn't really much for Will to disagree with. The moment it was over, Hailey stood up to shake hands with those around her, thanking them all for welcoming her so warmly. Before she could finish shaking the first hand, Will was up and on his way to the door. Needless to say, it did not leave a good impression with her; in fact, she felt he was going to be difficult to work with and although at the time she felt this was her dream job, she questioned whether she had the courage to work in an environment that bred such negativity. She shook it off and told herself one person can't possibly ruin it for her. Everyone else had seemed so warm and eager to work together and so she decided to ignore Will, who she pegged as just a jerk and enjoy her job. Little did she know, Will would change her life forever and on more than one occasion.

It was at an event for a campaign the company had just released that they had their first conversation. Hailey was at the bar waiting to order a drink when Will walked up and stood beside her. Instantly feeling nervous, she stood up straight and shrunk back a little. Looking at him from the corner of her eye, she couldn't help but notice how he seemed to have it all together in a way that was effortless. From the dark grey suit that looked like it cost an arm and a leg, but somehow he made look casual, to his dark brown, almost black hair that again, somehow looked like he had put all the effort in the world into, yet still somehow said he woke up, ran his fingers quickly through it and went on his way. She wanted to say hi and hopefully break the ice between them, but couldn't stop over thinking how to go about it and in the end, decided it had been too long already since he walked up next to her, that saying anything now would just make her look awkward.

Will raised his hand toward the bar staff; a gesture that seemed confident and well practiced and within seconds the bartender appeared. Hailey had been standing there for no less than ten minutes while others came and went and she couldn't so much as catch the bartender's eye.

"A beer. And for you?" he said as he looked from the server to Hailey.

Stunned that he had even noticed her, the words fell out of her mouth with a slight hint of confusion. "Uh, a rye and coke please."

The bartender smiled as if he was able to predict the future from this small encounter and began to get their drinks. Hailey started to open her black patent leather clutch in search of money but as she unsnapped the clasp, Will put his hand over hers and said, "Don't worry about it. I've got this one."

She felt a shock go through her when the warmth of his hand touched hers and she couldn't help but realize she was excited by it.

The bartender brought their drinks and Will paid. He turned, smiled at Hailey and walked away before she even had a chance to say thank you.

Maybe he wasn't such as ass after all.

Their encounters over the next few weeks were much like the one they had that evening. Short with very few words but they left something hanging. She couldn't quite put her finger on it but there was definitely more to this guy than he let on and slowly Hailey's nerves began to settle around him.

One Saturday, as she was sitting around her apartment in sweats, eating cereal for lunch and watching the one boring local channel she could actually get on her cable lacking tv, her phone rang.
"Hello?" she said as she put the phone to her ear.
"Hey, it's Will."
Silence. Dead silence was all she could muster. It felt like it lasted an awkwardly long time. Why was he calling her? How did he get her number? But really...why was he calling her!?
"Hi," she finally said with a bit of a nervous and confused tone to her voice.
"Listen, I'm stuck in town for a bit and I thought I remembered that you live close by. I wondered if maybe you could use some company for a few hours?"
Without thinking, she said yes, hung up the phone and looked up at the clock then looked down at herself. Panic set in and she ran to her room, grabbed a pair of jeans off the floor and a top out of the yet to be folded hamper; at least it was clean. He would be there in fifteen minutes and although her apartment was small, she wasn't expecting anyone and little piles of mess had built up. She didn't have a lot of time so she tossed the random loose clothes from the living room into her bedroom along with the gossip magazines from the coffee table and the dirty towels from the bathroom floor. As she

ran past the mirror she caught a glimpse of her unkempt weekend hair and stopped dead in her tracks. Messy bun it was, hoping to go for the cute relaxed look. She grabbed the bare basics from her makeup bag and gave her face a quick once over. Walked back into the living room only to hear a knock at the door, right on time. She took a deep breath and walked calmly to her front entranceway, paused and then unlocked and opened the door.

Over the next few weeks, Hailey found herself drawn to Will. When she had news, he was the first person she wanted to tell. Emails back and forth at all hours of the day and night, talking about nothing and everything all at the same time. They saw each other every moment they could but kept their growing friendship to a minimum while at work. Slowly she started to realize why he gave off such a strong and closed off impression. He wasn't an ass, he was just unhappy. He opened up to Hailey and told her things he had never told anyone before. He felt like he was taking two steps forward and one step back at work and while he idolized creativity, he felt it was squashed into a box within this company. He had already climbed high enough on the corporate ladder to know that starting over elsewhere would not necessarily be the best idea. He felt he needed to prove himself with a few good accounts and then hopefully change would come calling for him. It just seemed a vicious circle for the last while and it was wearing thin on his nerves. His marriage was less than perfect and he described it as a waiting game. He knew his wife was not the one he was meant to be with, but had married her out of guilt and presumed obligation. They had dated in high school and through college, off and on, but was again put in a box by her and everyone they knew that they were supposed to get married. It made it hard to walk away without feeling like he was letting everyone down or that it came out of nowhere. Since it wasn't like either one of them had done anything to truly warrant a separation and divorce, he felt he was simply waiting for the day he had reason to leave. That it would inevitably come, because how could any two people be truly happy when you are simply going through the motions? Then he could be free without all the fuss and blame being put solely on him. He knew it was probably a poor way to look at it but he wasn't a bad guy and didn't want to hurt anyone. He simply wanted to be free to live and be happy.

After he met Hailey, things had started to change. There was a spark and excitement there that he hadn't known before. He felt like she was waking up all of the parts of him that were lying dormant, just waiting for the right moment to stand up and scream THIS IS IT!

But neither one had actually said out loud how they felt about each other. She assumed, as did he, that the feeling was mutual but when you have the obvious obstacles in the way, his marriage and their age gap, neither one wanted to put the truth out there in words in case the other thought it was a bad idea. So they tiptoed around their flirtation, pushing the envelope so to speak, a little further each time they met or spoke.

One evening while they were working late at the office, they found themselves with dinner ordered in and shoes kicked off. They were supposed to be focused on a campaign for work, but after two hours of non-stop advertisement, Hailey grabbed a throw pillow from the leather sofa she was sitting on and threw it down at Will. He was seated on the floor with his back against the couch so he didn't see it coming. Hitting him in the side of the head, she began laughing while Will sat looking stunned before deciding to retaliate. He reached for the pillow that had landed in his lap and tossed it back at her. She put her arms up, still laughing and the pillow bounced back to the floor and out of reach for both of them. Realizing the only other pillow that was within either of their grasps was at the opposite end of the couch, they both dove for it with Hailey grabbing a hold of the corner before Will could get there. Without even thinking, he threw himself on top of her, pinning her so she couldn't hit him with the pillow, her arms up over her head, held by one of his hands. And just like that, the laughter stopped. It was as if everything just froze and nothing else mattered. His hand slowly slid from her hands, down her wrist and arm until he reached her side. Sliding his hand underneath the small of her back and leaning in close, she thought to herself, *this is it; he's actually going to kiss me* and she knew that she couldn't bring herself to stop him. He pulled back a bit and looked into her eyes; almost as if he was asking her permission without saying a word. Her left hand reached for the sides of his face, caressed his cheek and then gently she let her fingers slip over his ears and into his hair. It was all the permission he needed and with that, he leaned in and kissed her for the first time, pulling her body towards him so tightly it was as if any air between them would be too much.

In that kiss, they found something neither had ever found before. When their lips finally parted, all either could do was smile at each other. Partly because they were embarrassed that their true feelings were finally out there and partly because it was something they had both been holding themselves back from and to finally allow it, felt euphoric. The silence said more than any words could have in that moment and they both knew that this was only the beginning.

As if karma had been sitting right there in the room with them watching, Will's phone rang and the smile on his face disappeared. He sat up and reached for it on the coffee table where it was laying amongst their papers and take out dishes. Hailey knew who was calling and she kept her silence.

"Hey," he said, trying to sound as normal and happy to hear from her as he could. "Yea, most of the team has headed home already so I'm about to pack up and go. I shouldn't be long." He paused to listen to his wife on the other end. "I kno - I know. It's getting late. This is just a big campaign and we're in the finishing stages. No, this is the last late night..." his voice trailing off, realizing that by saying that, he essentially had no excuses for time away from the house to see where things would go with Hailey.

"Ya, I'll be home soon," he said. He hung up the phone, clenching it in his fist. With his head hanging low, he closed his eyes. Hailey didn't know if she should comfort him or keep her distance. She sat still, patiently waiting for him to make the first move. Hoping with everything she had in her that he could face her, that she would be the one comforted and reassured by him. It was selfish and she knew it. She never thought of herself as a bad person and even somehow, still in that moment, she didn't see herself as a cheater or a mistress or that she had even made a mistake. There was more right to the two of them together than she could even wrap her mind around. That had to speak for something. Giving in had to have been the right decision.

Will's eyes opened and his gaze drifted across the room. He sat up and turned towards Hailey. *Truth time* she thought.

"I don't know how to do this," he said.

She could feel heat rising through her body and tears building, although she was determined that she wouldn't let him see them.

"I don't know how, but I'm going to figure it out. Whatever just happened between us, what's obviously been happening between us...." his voice trailed off.

"Will, I..." she started

Before she could finish, he interrupted. "What's been happening between us is what's been missing my entire life. I always knew it was out there, I just never expected to find it so soon. I thought I was stuck. I thought... I thought I had to wait. I don't want to wait anymore. Jesus, I'm coming on strong." His eyes scanning the room out of nervousness. He didn't want to scare her off. They had literally just admitted they felt anything at all for each other and here he was going off about leaving his wife for her. Hailey had never seen him like this before, so vulnerable and scared. He was always so confident and in control.

She reached out for his hand and squeezed it tightly, hoping it would be enough to let him know she felt the same way, but not enough to make him feel pressured into doing something he wasn't comfortable with. Rarely did she ever find herself in the position to be the one calling all the shots, and she wasn't about to start now. This was bigger than her and she knew Will was the one with more to lose. This was his choice.

"Hailey, all I know is since the night at the bar, I haven't been able to stop thinking about you. I've told you things I've never told anyone and genuinely wanted you to know those things. I get excited when I know I'm going to see you. I check my email fifty times a day just hoping you've written back. For christ sake I smoke, but you make me want to quit. Being around you makes me want to be better. I know what I want. I've known it this entire time, I just...I guess I just don't know how to start."

"Well, kissing me was a good first step," she said with a coy smile hoping to lighten the mood.

"Yea, it was the best first start."

And there it was.

They knew that they would have to be careful. This had to be handled well but quickly. Neither one wanted anyone hurt but they knew that if they waited, if they tried to hide their relationship, inevitably, someone getting hurt was exactly what was going to happen.

They tidied the conference room they had been working in, put their shoes on, grabbed their things and headed for the door. When they both reached for the knob at the same time, their hands grazed against each other. It was like being a teenager all over again and feeling butterflies in your stomach. They smiled at each other and Hailey pulled her hand back. Will opened the door and with that, they were coworkers again.

Hailey made a quick stop at her desk to tidy up and as she slid her purse over her shoulder, Will, who had been waiting near the elevator, walked back toward her.

"It's late and dark out. I'll walk you to your car," he said.

She smiled and said "thanks" before looking away like they had an inside joke she was hoping to keep to herself.

The elevator ride took an eternity as they stood side by side in silence. Their hands dangling down at their sides, fingers so close they could almost touch. They both stared straight ahead as the elevator numbers counted down 11..10..9..8...

"Thanks for your help on the Bradford account tonight," he blurted. As if making small talk would somehow convince the guard, who would probably not pay attention to the security tape of two random people taking the elevator to the parking garage, that nothing was out of the ordinary.

"Of course. I think we have a real winner on our hands with this one. We make a good team. Besides, it was worth it. You know, for the Chinese food."

3..2..1.. The elevator stopped and the doors opened. The parking garage was close to empty, making it easy to spot her black pick up truck.

"That's me," she said nodding her head in the direction of her parking spot.

"A truck girl. I would not have guessed," he said, sounding surprised.

"Well, this city girl wasn't always a city girl. I guess you can take the girl out of the country but you can't always take the country out of the girl." Feeling like she had just said the dumbest thing she possibly could have mustered, she rolled her eyes and hoped he hadn't noticed.

"Well, have a good night. I'll see you tomorrow?" he asked.

"Ya," she said as she started toward her truck; fiddling with her keys, still embarrassed by her less than original small talk.

Will turned to walk towards his car, took about five steps and turned to face Hailey; walking backwards now he just smiled at her. He turned away, only to take a few more steps and turn to face her for the second time. By this time, she was standing beside her driver's side door, unable to take the next step to unlock and open the door to get in. She couldn't help but watch him sort out whether he was actually going to his car or not.

"Having a hard time leaving?" she yelled across the empty garage.

He stopped walking and paused. The moment seemed to take forever, then he finally broke the silence with, "You have no idea."

With that, he took a few steps toward her before breaking into a sprint. When he reached her he wasted no time in wrapping one arm around her waist and placing the other hand on her cheek, pushing her back against her truck. When his lips touched hers it was like electricity flew through her body. It was one of those moments every girl sees in the movies and daydreams about. You never actually expect it will happen in real life though, but here she was, in her magical movie moment being kissed by the leading guy who never should have looked her way.

He slowly pulled away from her, smiled and turned, running off to his car. She couldn't speak. She couldn't move. She just stood there, mouth parted with a half-cocked smile in absolute amazement.

Two

Nowhere Else To Go

Three weeks had passed since that night in the office and Hailey felt like her life was changing at lightning speed. She was on the phone with her Mom when she heard a knock at the door of her apartment. She opened it to find Will standing there with a duffle bag in his hand and a look of desperation on his face.

Shock overwhelmed her body as the reality of what she was seeing set in. "Mom, I'm going to have to call you back," she said, without taking her eyes off Will. She didn't even wait for a response. She just lowered the phone and hung up.

"What are you doing here?" she asked

Will simply shrugged his shoulders. "I don't have anywhere else to go".

He had left his wife and even though they both knew that had been the plan, neither one had any real idea of when or how it was going to happen.

Hailey opened the door wider and stepped aside to let him in. And that was the beginning of their life together.

They had decided it was best to keep things quiet between them at the office for the sake of unnecessary drama or judgment at how fast they got together after his separation, but at the apartment things were different. They soaked up each other's time and company, never seeming to be able to get enough. They would lie in bed together all night, almost afraid to fall asleep; both trying not to miss a single minute of their time together. They laughed and played together, cooked together and made love every chance they got, in every room they had. They couldn't keep their hands off each other. They also fought like neither one had ever fought with anyone before. Each hurt feeling or miscommunication seemed to hold more weight than they were used to. They yelled and slammed doors, even going as far as to walk out on each other. Giving each other the silent treatment for days on end became their norm when they argued, both hoping the other would break the silence and they could go back to being in love. Although they both hated the fights, Will thought it meant something was wrong with them. That maybe they weren't meant to be together after all, but Hailey said that she would be worried if they didn't fight.

"If we care enough to fight, that just means this is worth fighting for. If we didn't fight, then I'd be worried."

Life changes didn't stop there. Almost a year after they had started living together, Will found himself exhausted from such a fast-paced work life that still left him feeling like he was only spinning in circles and Hailey realized that advertising was just not the world she wanted to be in. She missed her roots and felt trapped living in the city.   Will had made the tough decision to shake things up a bit and applied for a teaching position at a local college on the outskirts of the city and when he got the call to say he landed the job; a position in the marketing and advertising department, they both quit their jobs at the firm and decided to move. They desperately wanted some living space and Hailey's childhood dream had always been to run her own farm, so they mapped out an area that would work for Will's commute to the college but give Hailey the space to live out her country farm dreams. After looking at a few places, they settled on the perfect piece of forever. A beautiful log farmhouse overlooking fields just waiting for horses to graze and a long dirt driveway that made its way from the road through the trees before opening up to their own personal slice of heaven. The barn was old but in good shape and was already set up with horse stalls. Just perfect for what Hailey wanted. All she really needed to do to the place was put in a chicken coop and a vegetable garden and they would be all set.

Packing up the apartment wasn't as easy as they thought it would be. It was the place everything really began for them. They had spent most of their relationship until that point hiding away there just the two of them, so saying goodbye was hard. With tears welling up in her eyes, Hailey took one last look before closing the door and walking away. Will put his arm around her shoulders and held her as they walked to the office mail slot to drop their keys off.

"Chapter one complete," he said with a smile.

Hailey looked up at him and nodded once. "I think chapter two is going to be amazing."

Three

The Farm

    The first few years on the farm were, for the most part, everything Hailey could have wished for. She had found Charlie, a beautiful buckskin mare; adopted a couple of dogs from the local shelter and when she wasn't out with them and the chickens on the farm, she was in the house, tucked away at her desk overlooking the fields and working on her other passion - writing. Instead of

looking for a job in town or driving back and forth into the city every day like Will did, she had decided to pursue her dream of being a writer and since she had never felt inspiration for life anywhere like she did when she was on the farm, she ran with it. Her first book did well enough to allow her to continue and with Will's teaching salary, they were doing okay for themselves.

What wasn't doing okay was their relationship, at least in Hailey's eyes. They weren't in any danger of splitting up, but Hailey couldn't help but feel like Will had just become content and the motivation to put effort into their relationship had dwindled. They had been together about three years before the fights focused on their future. Hailey wanted to eventually get married but Will didn't see the point. He had already had that piece of paper and in the end, it hadn't meant anything at all. It just caused him stress when he had to get out of it. Hailey took that as him having one foot out the door of their relationship, a trait she couldn't help but notice she had seen in him before, and look how well that had worked out. With that always in the back of her mind, she didn't even dare discuss the idea of having babies with him, at least not yet. In her heart, she already knew his answer to that. She knew she wanted children but she also knew that with Will, she had to resign herself to his timeline if she even had a chance at him changing his mind. Pushing him before he was ready would just have him put up more roadblocks. To top it all off, Will's parents had never fully warmed up to her, and although they tried to be polite, it was obvious that they didn't see why he had left his first wife and thought this relationship was just some sort of mid-life crisis for Will. It hurt Hailey that they never really showed much interest in truly getting to know her and it definitely didn't help that in the beginning they would 'accidentally' call her by his ex's name or talk about moments they had all spent together

as a family, as if Hailey wasn't right there. Will had also
started teaching some evening classes at the college so he
was gone more and more, leaving Hailey feeling like their
lives were beginning to separate. She loved Will more
than she ever thought she could love anyone but she felt
alone most of the time and although she couldn't actually
imagine Will leaving, she felt like they may end up
spending the rest of their lives living like roommates.
They just weren't laughing much anymore. They tended
to go about their own way when they were both in the
house and when they did spend time together it was
usually in front of the tv. So on the sixth anniversary of
the night they first kissed, the only anniversary Hailey
ever thought she would get to celebrate, she told herself
not to get her hopes up. In the past, she always wondered
if Will would propose. This time she knew better and just
tried to enjoy the evening with him and the fact that he
was willing to celebrate anything at all. She knew Will
wasn't a bad guy, he just sometimes only saw what he
wanted to see and although he loved Hailey deeply, he
had a hard time truly showing her in a way that let her
know she still meant something to him. In his mind, the
fact that they were together said enough. He didn't think
to show her how he felt with a lingering touch for no real
reason other than to be close to her or to take her hand
when they were walking. Those things had sort of faded
over time and that, along with all of the hours they spent
apart, left Hailey feeling like she wasn't truly that special
to him any longer.

They didn't have any real plans for their
anniversary, just to have a nice dinner and Hailey hoped,
maybe some sort of closeness that didn't result in them

ending up with the tv on. She had asked Will what he wanted to do a few weeks in advance and when he had more or less shrugged and said it was up to her, she decided to just keep it simple. The evening went on and although Hailey was glad she didn't expect too much, she realized that with each passing perfect moment where Will didn't propose, somewhere inside her she felt a twinge of sadness. Realizing she couldn't fully shake the hope that he might just surprise her, she tried to shove her hurt feelings down. Out of sight, out of mind, at least for Will. She didn't see much point in hoping he would notice she was hurting and feel guilty. The last thing she wanted was a proposal out of pity, nor did she want to ruin their evening.

It was close to eight o'clock that night when Will said he heard something outside and stepped out on the front porch to listen better.

Well that's that, she thought to herself.

She started to straighten up around the living room when Will hollered in that he thought a coyote was out there and she had better come out and bring Charlie into the barn. Charlie was honestly Hailey's best friend and the thought of her being in danger made Hailey sick. She dropped the throw pillows and ran out the front door, leaving the screen door swinging behind her. She was about to blow right past Will and down the steps heading for the field when the ground fell out from under her feet. Will dropped down on one knee as she approached him and held a tiny black box out, open in her direction. He wasn't really the type to express his feelings to well so he didn't open with any long romantic story or praise of their relationship. He simply waited until he had her attention, and asked her to marry him.

Hailey stood in complete and utter shock. "Are you serious!?" she asked.

"Yea, of course I am," he said smiling at her like her shock was exactly what he had planned.

"But...but you don't want to get married. You've been really clear on that."

"Can't a guy change his mind? I changed my mind!" He shrugged his shoulders like it was the most natural thing in the world for him to have just woken up one day and decided he did actually want to get married.

Hailey just stood staring at him in disbelief. She couldn't wrap her mind around how this was really happening. "This is real? You're serious?"

Will laughed, "yes, I'm serious."

Looking down at the ring and then back to Will's eyes, Hailey dropped to the ground on her knees and wrapped her arms around his neck, nearly knocking them both over in the process.

"YES!" she cried. "Of course I'll marry you!" With tears streaming down her face she clung to him like she was afraid to let go in case it was just a dream.

They had a small wedding the next fall right there on their farm and it seemed to give them a renewed sense of their love for each other. Will, without hesitation or being asked, took time off work after the wedding for a honeymoon at home. They woke up each morning together for coffee on the porch followed by barn chores and a walk with the dogs. Now granted, Hailey did the majority of the barn chores, but Will was right there with her and didn't mind helping out with cleaning up a stall if it needed it. They made love in the middle of the day and played board games most nights instead of watching tv.

Instinctively, Hailey knew things would settle again
and more than likely once Will went back to work, things
would go back to being quite a bit less about them as a
couple but at least she knew that Will was fully
committed. She wasn't sure what had changed in him
but she wasn't about to press her luck by asking. She
just tried to soak it all up while she could and hoped that
at least a little bit of his newfound ability to show how
much he cared for her would stick around.

It had been six months since the wedding and
Hailey found that as long as they weren't in the midst of
an argument, Will was more open to talking about his
feelings if she asked him to, rather than just keeping it all
in, and she became more comfortable telling him what she
needed from him without worrying that she was about to
start a war. But, as she had expected they would, most
things sort of fell back into old habits and routine.
Hailey tried to accept that they both just needed different
things from each other and since Will had gone against
everything he said he would by asking her to marry him,
she figured it was her turn to swallow her pride and try
and change her idea of what she felt she needed from him.
Slowly she became more accepting of the idea that they
could make it even though they were very different people.
Will still had a soft spot for city living and didn't
mind the commute to and from work or weekends away
for teaching courses. Hailey had taken a while to admit it
but eventually accepted that she was a country girl
through and through and felt alive when she was on the
farm. She didn't like heading into the city for anything
and rarely did. She had found pretty decent success as a
novelist but since she wasn't really willing to leave the

farm for weeks on end for book tours and signings, she kept her career as a writer more or less sitting on the edge of something great. She didn't get into it in the first place to become known around the world, she simply had a few stories to tell and found a way to tell them. She was glad that people wanted to read her work and she was more than happy to sign books to be sent away when requested. She had built a following of dedicated readers who she was quite open with about her desire to keep life simple and do the things she enjoyed. Things she couldn't quite do if she was always away on tours.

The farm was running well thanks to Hailey's hard work and Will's desire to support her in all her efforts. She had gone from a small egg and garden set up that took care of their own personal needs to expanding enough to join in the town's local farmers market and provide goods to the community. Being a fairly shy and quiet person, it allowed her to meet people she wouldn't otherwise have met. This was how she met Amanda, a woman from town about Hailey's age who she felt an instant connection with.

Amanda lived right in town with her boyfriend Collin and their two boys but longed for a quieter and simpler life and took every spare opportunity she had to help Hailey out with country living. The two women had bumped into each other a few times at the farmers market before Hailey had joined as a vendor and had begun a friendship. Amanda had become Hailey's proofreader for her novels, even before any editors had the chance to get their hands on her work and when it was farmers market season, Amanda was always there to lend a helping hand. Hailey would watch the boys when Amanda and Collin needed a sitter and when Colin had proposed, Hailey was the first person Amanda had called.

Hailey knew that she was living a dream. She had a husband who loved her, a few close friends that supported her and the peace and quiet she had always dreamt of. She didn't want to take it for granted in the least, but deep down inside she knew there was still something missing. She could never quite put her finger on it, she just felt that there was something more for her out there somewhere. She was never one to think that you should ever just be content with life. She wanted to be someone who was always looking to learn something new or have goals for her future and because of that, she had a hard time accepting that at barely thirty years old, this was it for her. So she held onto the hope that one day, something would surprise her and take her down a path she hadn't seen coming.

Four

Out Of Nowhere

Hailey went out to the barn at eight forty-five Thursday morning in order to bring Charlie in and get her all cleaned up for her farrier's visit at nine thirty. It was the middle of August so the morning air was already starting to warm up for the day. Although she wasn't a fan of waking up and needed about a pot and a half of coffee to feel like she was ready to move, mornings were actually her favourite time of day. She loved being out and about when the world was still quiet.

Hailey had found it difficult to find a new farrier when her's had up and left before the beginning of summer. She had contacted at least seven other farriers in the area and either never heard back from them or was told they weren't taking on new clients. Jamie had been the only one to say he'd be able to come out, but after asking around about him, she wasn't sure what to expect. She didn't know too many people in the horse world close enough to get a real opinion from, but the few that she did ask hinted at the idea that although he was good with the horses, he was a little more into himself that anyone really cared for. She heard the nickname "hot Jamie" more than once and was told that he was one of those guys that knew people thought it and used it to his advantage. All she knew was that even though he had agreed to take on her horse, he had annoyed her right off the bat by not being as organized as she was used to. Setting a date and time for Charlie's trim was like pulling teeth. Writing him, then waiting days with no response just to write again and get what felt like a very laid back, half-assed answer was not her idea of a good working relationship. She liked things to be clear and Jamie was proving to be the opposite of that.

Nine-thirty rolled on well past into ten o'clock, still with no sign of him. Thinking to herself this was enough of a frustration that no matter how right everyone else may have been about his looks, no charms this guy could throw out would be enough to win her over in that way.

Finally, at a quarter to eleven she heard the sound of a truck pulling up the lane; an hour and fifteen minutes late. She toyed with the idea of having at him about being on time for their next appointment but put that idea on the back burner realizing not only would she probably be too shy to actually say anything, but she also decided it was better to be the bigger person and assume there was a good reason, at least this time.

She heard the truck door shut and the sound of footsteps scuff in the dirt out front of the barn.

"Hey, how's it going?" he said with a country as hell accent. He walked in through the open barn door, took a few steps towards her and held out his hand. "I'm Jamie."

In that moment, she felt dumbstruck. She hadn't expected it nor would she have even believed her own story if she told it, but somehow, with just that simple introduction, the way he spoke and his confidence, how he made and held eye contact with her without making her feel shy or awkward like she usually would have....she was sold. No one had ever changed her mind that fast or that easily and it left her shell shocked.

"Hailey," she said with a smile, trying not to stutter over her own name. Reaching for his hand she added, "Glad you made it all the way out here on such short notice."

"Sorry about being late," he said. "I had to squeeze a trim in before heading out here and it took a little longer than expected. Not a horse I'm lookin' forward to doin' again to tell ya the truth."

The rational part of her brain couldn't help but think a call or text ahead of time would have been helpful, but she mentally gave him a pass and accepted the excuse against all her better judgement.

"Well, this is Charlie and she should go pretty easy on you. She's never given anyone trouble that I've seen.

She is however in need of a good trim and has some nasty chips on one hoof. She was due a few weeks ago but my old farrier moved and didn't give me much of a heads up. Left me in a bit of a pinch."

Jamie put his hand on Charlie's back hip and ran it along her flank towards her front shoulder as he walked along her. "It's this one here?" he asked.

Hailey nodded and sort of let out a mumbled 'mhmm'.

Jamie picked up Charlie's hoof and Hailey couldn't help but realize over and over again that all her disdain for poor communication and how late he was had completely vanished. She had no real reason why; he had been there for a mere two minutes, but she could already tell that she wished she had a few more horses for him to trim to make the appointment last longer. Of course, he was gorgeous like everyone said. Hot Jamie was an obvious and ridiculously accurate nickname for him. He was around the same age as Hailey, quite tall with light brown hair and a crooked smile that sort of drew a person in. Hailey found herself waiting for the nervousness to set in and the moment where she didn't know what to say to him, but for some reason that never really happened. He put her at complete ease and seemed wholeheartedly interested in what she had to say. Hailey wasn't exactly the most confident person in the world and she was happily married but for the first time since meeting Will, she felt that spark of interest in someone and the enjoyment of being focused on. She obviously wouldn't act on anything and assumed the moment was fleeting, but she realized she sort of liked the feeling of being curious about a guy again. There was a magic in the idea of having that little something for herself, something that in the end, was harmless, but gave her moments to look forward to from time to time.

Will was a good husband, but over the years she learned he was insecure about himself to a point and although he would never admit it, he was jealous of men he thought would catch Hailey's attention and this guy fit the bill to a T. She knew she would have to keep her conversations about Charlie's trims to a minimum with Will in case he got any wrong ideas.

Jamie stood up and turned to Hailey. "The chip looks bad but it's not actually causing any harm."

"Oh perfect!" Hailey said with a smile. "I was worried we were getting into some trouble."

While Jamie headed out to his trailer to get his tools, Hailey put her hands on Charlie's nose and ran her finger tips along her soft muzzle. "Wow," she whispered, as she tried to subdue the smile that had yet to leave her face before he came back.

Jamie walked back in and made small talk easy for twenty minutes until Charlie's trim was done and he began to pack up his tools. "That's that. She looks great and we'll get those flat feet of hers rounded up with another trim or two. She'll be as good as new."

Hailey could drown in that accent. That, matched with his warm brown eyes and red tee shirt that clung to all the right places was enough to make her sink and never come back up again!

"Shake it off!" she whispered to herself. Not understanding how in such a short time this guy who she started off not really liking had not only won her over but had piqued an interest in her that hadn't happened since she met her husband. She was attracted to him and was shocked at the entire situation.

Hailey thanked him as he picked up the rest of his tools and she handed him the money she owed him.

"I'll get ya booked in for another six weeks or so," he said as he headed for the door.

Hailey thanked him on his way out and then grabbed her saddle thinking tacking up for a ride would be a good distraction.

"Whew, look at that piece of leather. That's a beauty of a saddle right there."

Hailey had no idea Jamie had come back in the barn, thank goodness she hadn't said anything to Charlie that he would have overheard. He walked around to where she was fiddling with her stirrup and said, "use a broom."

"A broom?" she asked, not understanding what he was talking about.

"Yea." He walked over and picked up the stirrup hanging from Charlie's side. Standing only inches from her, Hailey found herself looking more intently at his hands than at what he was trying to show her. She couldn't help but notice they were the hands of a working man, strong and toughened.

"When you put your saddle on the rack, stick a broom handle in the stirrups to train the leather to bend." He bent the fender to show her what he meant. "It's a pain, at least I find it a pain when they lay flat, so I use a broom handle to turn them."

She looked at him dumbfounded. She felt like such an amateur standing next to him and wondered if he thought less of her for it. Somehow he had managed to pick out the one thing that had actually caused her frustration and it felt a little close for comfort.

Saddles felt personal to her, it's the connection between you and your horse and she knew a rider with as much experience as Jamie would feel the same way too. The fact that he made a point of letting her know he liked hers and offered advice on it just felt a little close. Almost to close for someone she had just met about thirty minutes ago. This guy was good at what he did and he knew it. She had a feeling he damn well knew he could be as late as he wanted to most any job and make up for it with his far too easy to enjoy company. Maybe everyone was right about him after all. Although at the moment, Hailey really didn't care.

"Thanks, that's actually been bugging me to be honest. I never thought to use a broom handle. I'll give it a shot."

With a coy smile on his face, he took a couple of steps backwards. "Alright then, you have a good day...and a good ride." He nodded his head in an old cowboy tipping your hat kind of way.

"Thanks," she said almost too innocently.

"I'll see ya next time Darlin', " he said as he stepped out and vanished toward his truck.

Hailey nearly stumbled over herself at the sound of him calling her 'Darlin'. Thinking that men like that just don't exist anymore, "Where did this guy come from?" she whispered to herself.

The engine started and she listened to the truck drive down the laneway and head out. That was the longest yet shortest half hour of her life and she had no idea what she was going to tell Will when he inevitably asked her how it went.

Five

Undeniable

Winter had been long and Hailey's first assumption about Jamie's appointment keeping skills only proved to be right with every trim. Although, so did his ability to make her forget all about it with each and every visit. Appointments would get pushed back by days or sometimes even a week or so and on the days he finally got there, he was always far later than he said he would be. Leaving her to put her day on pause, waiting around for him to get there. Will questioned why she didn't just fire him and find a new farrier since he caused her such a headache every time she needed him to come out, but

each time the conversation came up she found herself
spouting off some line about loyalty and giving him a
chance since he always did a great job once he was there.
She made excuses for him by saying that she was only
one quick stop for him in a full roster of horses and that
of course, he would simply be trying to fit her in when he
could. That her horse wasn't a sport horse, nor did she
wear shoes so it wasn't like she needed to be race or show
ready all the time. She was an easy keeper in that way
and Jamie was probably doing the best he could with the
amount of work and little time he had. Will seemed to
buy the excuses and Hailey tried to choke back the idea
that in reality, she simply didn't want to fire him because
she enjoyed the times he did come out far more than she
should. She liked the ease of small talk with him, and no
matter how nervous she was about coming up with the
right thing to say, he always seemed fully interested and
carried the conversation when she couldn't during those
twenty-minute visits. The fact that he smelled so good it
nearly made her speechless and the sound of his voice
with that southern drawl didn't help matters any. Even
though it should have been a business type decision, she
had made it a very personal one. She liked his visits and
so she chose to hold onto that, even though she did
everything in her power to make herself believe the stories
and excuses she gave Will. Of course, she felt guilty but
convinced herself that it was all harmless and didn't
jeopardize anything. She told herself there must be plenty
of times that Will had crushes or harmless interest in
other women at the college that he never told her about,
allowing herself to somehow validate her wandering
interest. She spent most of her time alone anyway, it was
sort of nice to have something, even if it was just in her

head, that no one else knew about. Her own little enjoyable secret.

Aside from the obvious fun of it all, she had started to see something in Jamie that she figured most people simply overlooked. He wasn't nearly as cocky as she had originally thought or how everyone made him out to be. Instead, she started to think it was more of something he tried to put out there, simply because it was the part everyone always expected him to play, like he had somehow been stuck in a box by the people in his world and he simply didn't feel like he had the choice to break free. She sometimes felt like he was sad or a little lost and Hailey liked that during their short conversations she was able to see his mood change to something a little brighter and over time, a little less forced. She realized for all the talking he must do in a day with clients, that it didn't seem he often got to talk about anything that mattered. The weather, the horses and more than likely, all about his clients days were obviously the forced topics of conversation. She didn't get the impression a lot of people asked him how he was, how his day was going or what he was interested in. Hailey had always been empathetic to other people, a bonus of being the shy girl that kept to herself. She was able to take the time to really try and see people and so she had tried to ask Jamie a little about himself with each visit. Regardless of how much she enjoyed looking at him, she figured everyone deserves to feel like their thoughts and experiences matter. She hoped that if she was right about him, she was able to make even a small difference to him.

The first Sunday of May had rolled around and the market in town was gearing up for a busy summer.

Hailey was looking forward to it, in fact, she was craving it. There was just something very old fashion about it that made her feel at home. Neighbours coming together to provide for each other was just something that felt right to her and she was excited to be a part of it.

Amanda swung by the house early that morning to help Hailey load the cartons of vegetables and eggs in the truck before they headed in to set up on the main street.

The crowds of people always started out slow but by mid-morning it was a steady stream of locals buying up goods to get them through the week until the next market.

As Hailey finished chit chatting with an older gentleman from town who had been teaching her all about the town's farming history, she heard a voice with the most perfect subtle country twang. "Fancy seeing you here," she heard the voice say.

Goosebumps instantly covered her skin as she turned toward the sound of his voice.

"Jamie Sutton, you don't really strike me as the farmers market type," she said smiling at him and trying to hide the fact that she might seem just a little too happy to see him.

"Ya, well I guess I'm not really. Amy wanted to come, so here I am." He sort of shrugged his shoulders with his answer and walked under Hailey's tent, browsing what she had on the table for sale.

The smile fell right off Hailey's face at the thought that his wife was somewhere nearby. Not that she thought there was anything more than an acquaintance relationship between them, but the idea of him with a wife sort of ruined the excitement of 'hot Jamie' or at least made Hailey hesitate with a different kind of guilt.

"Ah, I see," she paused and then with a mildly annoyed and somewhat involuntary sarcastic tone she asked, "Where is the Mrs.?"

Whether he caught onto the hint that Hailey had no desire to meet his wife or not, he laughed ever so slightly and said, "Oh, she's caught up somewhere talking so I'm wandering around on my own waiting for her to be done." And then changing the subject, "looks like you're doing well today."

With two hours left until it was time to pack up, Hailey was down to a few cartons of eggs and very little in the way of vegetables.

"Yea, I think I underestimated how much to bring. It's been busy today. Hope it keeps up this way for the summer."

"Well, I guess I know where to get my eggs from now on. Although I suppose that means I'll have to come to this every weekend." He reached for his wallet, pulling it out of the back pocket of his jeans and grabbed a few dollar bills. He picked up a carton of eggs and held the money out to Hailey.

Taking the bills, she looked him in the eye. "Well, you can always pop by the house during the week if the market isn't really your thing."

Amanda, who had been paying close attention to the conversation, shot Hailey a surprised look.

"Keep the change. See ya next Sunday," he said with a smirk as he turned and walked away.

Hailey took a deep breath and held onto the grin that always seemed to find it's way to her face when that man was around.

"Ummm, excuse me...who and what was that!?" Amanda asked as she swatted Hailey's shoulder in disbelief.

"That was Jamie and it was nothing. He's my farrier."

"If it's nothing, then why are you still smiling?"

Still holding the money he had handed her, Hailey laughed. "It's nothing; honestly."

Suddenly she had a new found excitement for the Sunday farmers market.

Jamie made it back to his truck to wait for his wife and from where he was parked, he had a pretty good view of Hailey's tent. He found himself staring at her and hoping Amy would take a little while to get back. Something about Hailey had grabbed his attention and although he couldn't quite place it, he couldn't stop watching her. It wasn't like he didn't notice she was attractive the first time he ever popped out to her farm, but he had lots of attractive clients, he just never paid much attention to that sort of thing. Something about seeing Hailey outside of their usual way took him by surprise.

The week went by fast and before Hailey knew it, it was Sunday morning. Her feet hit the floor before the sun came up and she was ready to go.

"What set the fire in you this morning?" Will asked as he groggily walked to the coffee pot.

"What do you mean? It's market day. I just wanted to be prepared. We came up a little short last week so I wanted to get a head start this morning and make sure we are ready." Realizing she was maybe a little too excited for the farmers market, she hoped this was enough to make both Will and herself believe her excuses.

As usual, Amanda showed up to help load the truck and they headed for the market. They no sooner got the tent set up and the food on the table before the rain started. At first, it was just a few sprinkles and nothing to worry too much about. But before long it started to pick up and everyone began packing up their goods and tents and heading out. Hailey's heart sank a little at the thought of not seeing Jamie. She wasn't even sure he would actually even show up, but just the thought that he might, had her feeling like she was spinning in circles all week long. Amanda ran back to the truck to grab the rest of the crates while Hailey packed up the ones they had tucked under the table. The wind was starting to blow and the tent was no longer keeping her totally dry.

"Does this mean I can't get eggs today?" a voice called from behind her. She stood up straight, resting her hands on the last bundle of carrots she had put in the crate. In an instant, she could care less about the bad weather and the failed market day. She turned around to see him standing in the rain, smiling at her. Jamie stepped toward her and under the tent to get out of the heavy rain.

"I've got your eggs right here, but the price just went up. Here's a crate, keep your money and get packin'!" she said.

Without a thought, he took the crate and got to work. Amanda came back with the rest of the crates, sided up next to Hailey and under her breath said "just nothing eh? Still sticking with that story are we?"

By the time they got the tent taken down and the truck loaded they were all soaking wet and the rain was showing no signs of slowing.

Hailey grabbed a carton of eggs and handed it to Jamie. "Honestly, thank you so much for helping."

"Well it didn't look like I had much of a choice if I wanted these," he said, taking the carton from her hands.

"I guess I did sort of force you into that, didn't I? I hope your wife isn't still back there waiting on you in the rain somewhere?"

"No no. She didn't come with me. She headed into the city early this morning. I was just sitting at home trying to make up some breakfast and realized I was fresh out of eggs, so here I am."

If she didn't know any better, she would have assumed that sounded like an excuse to see her and she secretly hoped that was the case.

The truth was, he hadn't really intended on coming to the market; the thought had crossed his mind a few times during the week, but he kept telling himself if he just didn't bother going, whatever it was about this girl would eventually fade. He was human after all, so it wasn't a total shock to him that he felt a slight interest in her. For some reason though, after his wife left the house that morning, he found himself sort of pacing back and forth with the idea of heading to the market growing stronger with every step. Each time he tried to tell himself to find something else to do, he found himself one step closer to the door. He finally gave in and grabbed his keys, hoping to not look overly obvious by showing up a second weekend in a row.

"Well, thank you again. I really..." her voice cut out when she felt a nudge in the rib from Amanda... "I mean *we*, we really appreciate the help."

"Yes, thanks! Jamie is it? I'm Amanda by the way. Haven't had the chance to actually be introduced yet."

"Hey, good to meet ya," he said reaching out his hand to shake Amanda's. "Alright ladies, I'm heading out if ya'll are set here?"

"Yea for sure, thanks again, Jamie." The sound of his name trailing off her lips made Hailey feel warm despite the rain. She knew she had let the idea of him get to her and go too far but she just couldn't seem to shake the thoughts. Things weren't wrong at home with Will. She was happy and loved him very much. She knew she had no real reason to need or want anything else. Jamie just seemed to excite a whole other part of her that she didn't know was there. The part of her that couldn't stop smiling about the thought of him showing up at the farmers market was not the part of her that got excited when she knew Will was getting home a few hours early on a Friday night and they would have dinner together. She was starting to feel like two entirely different people and didn't know what to do about it.

Jamie's drive home that morning had him smiling from ear to ear. He kept replaying the moment Hailey had realized he was behind her in his mind. The way she reacted made him think she was more confident than she usually let on and yet she came across as playful and sweet at the same time.

He had tried to keep himself under control, they both were married after all, but he couldn't stop himself from noticing how the rain had soaked Hailey's clothes and made her tee shirt cling to her. It was everything he could do to keep from staring and he hoped she hadn't noticed his eyes wandering. The last thing he wanted to do was come across as a creep or make her uncomfortable, but he couldn't ignore the fact that regardless of his attempts to act like it was nothing, he was growing more and more attracted to Hailey with each passing day.

Six

Crossing Lines

The summer was nearing its end and Hailey couldn't help but look back on it as one of her best yet. Her latest book has surpassed the sales goal she had set for it and to top it off, Jamie had continued to appear at the farmers market most Sundays, never staying longer than it took to buy eggs, but always leaving Hailey with questions about what she was thinking and why she felt this crazy excitement every time she heard his voice or saw him coming. Amanda had continued on her quest to figure out what was going on and never missed an opportunity to grill Hailey once Jamie had walked away each time. Hailey stuck to her story though and insisted she had no interest in him outside of casual friends or acquaintances.

Funny enough though, she couldn't help but notice that even though Jamie managed to make it to the market almost every Sunday morning, he still couldn't manage to make it to the appointments he set with her to trim Charlie on time. He was still either late or pushed things back by days, sometimes even a week.

The reality was, even though Jamie was starting to like their appointments a little more than he should, he didn't mind having an opportunity to chat with Hailey a few extra times in order to reschedule when things inevitably got busy, which with how overbooked he had allowed himself to be, it really wasn't a surprise to him that he was constantly having to rearrange clients and appointments. Besides, he found it sort of attractive the way he could tell she was super frustrated but tried to stay polite. She had a feisty side and he was sort of tempting fate in order to get to see it.

It was exactly one year until Amanda's big day and she had to finalize details with the venue and minister. She was farther ahead of most brides when it came to planning her wedding since she insisted on having everything done months in advance. She said she wanted to be able to just relax and enjoy herself when the day finally arrived and she wouldn't be able to do that if she was still planning until the last minute. She had asked Hailey to watch the boys for the afternoon and Hailey thought it would be a good distraction since Jamie was supposed to come by just before dinner for Charlie's trim, that is if he didn't call to change things up again. She was trying to get her head straight about him and figured the busier she kept on the days he was there the better.

Amanda dropped the boys just after lunch, kissed them goodbye and headed out.

"Be good for Hailey you two!" she hollered as she closed the car door and drove off.

"Alright, it's hot out today. Don't suppose you boys feel like a water gun fight huh?!" Hailey said as the boy's jaws dropped and they yelled "YA!!!"

She pointed towards the grass at the side of the front porch where she had already filled a blue kiddie pool with water and had laid out three super soakers for them to pick from. Running over and grabbing the leftover gun on the ground, she chased after them, everyone laughing and shooting each other with water. Hailey had on a pair of cut off jean shorts and a plain light blue ribbed tank top with flip flops to match. She stopped to kick off the sandals realizing they were too slippery in the now soaking wet grass and the boys, of course, took advantage of the situation and ganged up on her, both spraying her with water at the same time.

She ran toward the laneway hoping to be faster than a seven and four year old so she could regroup, when she saw Jamie's truck pull up. Not only had she not heard him coming, but for the first time in history, he was hours early.

She looked down at herself, standing there soaking wet with a super soaker in her hands before looking back up at Jamie and making eye contact with him. "Great, just great," she said to herself under her breath.

The sight of her soaking wet and totally unprepared to see him made Jamie smile. He pulled up next to the barn and opened the door to get out.

"Guess I should have called," he said with a laugh as he stepped out of the truck, closing the door.

"Would have been helpful." Hailey raised the water gun and shot a quick spray of water his way. If she was going to get caught playing, she might as well make the best of it she thought.

"Really?!" he said with a surprised look, tossing his arms out to the side. There was that fire he knew was inside her.

"I'm sorry," she said with a coy laugh. "You're working, that was a bad idea. Actually, I'm not really that sorry." She aimed and shot water toward him again.

The boys stood behind her laughing, having no idea who this guy was that just showed up out of nowhere or why Hailey thought it was a good idea to shoot him with a water gun.

"What's your name?" he asked as he pointed towards the younger of the two boys behind Hailey.

"Noah," he said, still laughing.

"Noah, mind if I borrow that water gun for a minute?"

"No no, that's not part of the plan," Hailey said with a concerned look on her face. "I'm sorry, I promise, I won't do it again." Laughing she whispered "oh shit!" as Noah walked over and handed Jamie the gun.

Hailey started walking backwards with her hands up as Jamie raised the water gun and aimed. A steady stream of water hit her legs and she started to run in circles trying to avoid it. "Jamie!!!" she hollered with a laugh and she dropped her gun while trying to get away. The boys chased after her, reaching out to try and grab her arms to hold her still. But it was a much larger hand that finally caught her. Suddenly she felt two strong arms wrap around her from behind, pinning her arms down and holding her still. She tried to slip out from his grip and get away but when she lowered herself he quickly grabbed hold of her by the waist, wrapping both arms around her in a bear hug.

"Get 'er boys!" he yelled.

Noah and Cooper came running, spraying Hailey as she fought helplessly to squirm her way out of Jamie's arms, secretly loving every second she spent being held by him. Having the boys take on the job of getting Hailey with the water guns had given Jamie a moment to focus on how it felt to hold her in his arms. They had never been that close before, nor could he really remember a time when they had actually touched more than hands grazing as they exchanged money for Charlie's trims or eggs at the market. He liked the feeling of her body held against his and wrapping his arms around her. She was trying to wiggle away, but he couldn't help but wonder if it was more for show than actually trying to get away. He wasn't holding her that tight after all.

At last, the guns were out of water and Jamie loosened his grip to allow Hailey to free herself. She let go of his arms, not realizing she had been holding onto him just as much as he had been holding her; she wiped the water off her face and felt his hands slip away from her waist. She took a few steps forward and turned to face him. When she noticed how wet he had ended up getting while trying to hold her still for the boys, she laughed slightly and said, "Looks like your plan kind of backfired there cowboy."

Had she just inadvertently given him a nickname? Embarrassed, she sort of hoped he would find it cute.

"Well, I'm not going to complain on a hot day like today," he said. "Besides, it was well worth it."

She assumed he meant because he got her back, but she couldn't help but let it pop into her head that just maybe he meant because he got to touch her.

As the boys busied themselves on the front porch with some toy trucks, Hailey got Charlie out of her stall and put her in the cross ties to let Jamie get to work.

She stood outside to keep an eye on the boys but couldn't help but quietly watch Jamie work away just inside the barn doors.

When he was done, he packed everything up and made a quick joke about making sure to call next time before saying goodbye to the boys and heading out. He was just about out of sight with the dust from the laneway flying up behind his trailer, when he stuck his hand out the window and waved goodbye. A sight Hailey had grown to expect and look for. This was the first appointment where they didn't really talk much while he worked but that visit left more confusion on Hailey's mind than anything. She had been trying everything to shake the thoughts of him, but every time she saw him it seemed to get worse and being held in his arms, feeling his body against hers, well, it didn't exactly do anything to get that kind of thinking off her mind.

Jamie wasn't any better off on his drive out and realized he was letting this girl get to him more than he should. He was glad he had rearranged his day to stop by Hailey's before some of his other clients, since he couldn't see how he would manage to go home to his wife after knowing what thoughts were crossing his mind; holding another woman that he couldn't seem to stop thinking about; he needed the day to shake himself back to reality. He was getting himself into a situation he wasn't sure how to handle, but stuffed the guilt down, telling himself it was harmless, or at least wouldn't go anywhere since they were both married and it would eventually just fade away.

When Amanda swung by to pick the boys up later that afternoon at the farm, Hailey had hoped they would keep the water fight story to themselves, but of course, her luck wasn't that good.

"MOM!" Noah yelled as Amanda came into the house. "Hailey shot some guy then he grabbed her and Cooper and I shot them both until they were soaked!"

"Umm, what?" Amanda asked as she glanced Hailey's direction with a confused look.

"Yea. We had a water gun fight to cool off." Hoping that was enough to shut the conversation down and move on, Hailey walked to the fridge. "Stay for dinner?" she asked.

"No, sorry, we can't tonight. Collins' car is in the shop so we have to pick him up from work. Wait, what guy did you shoot?"

Hailey tried not to smile since she knew exactly how Amanda would react, but it was no use.

"Hailey Jenkins are you kidding me?!" Amanda yelled.

"It's nothing. I swear. It's nothing."

"Yea right. Nothing my ass. You watch yourself there missy before you get yourself wound up in a heap of trouble you can't get yourself out of."

Hailey nodded in a yes ma'am kind of way and then helped the boys collect their things and hugged them both before they ran out to the car.

"I've got my eye on you," Amanda said as she stepped out on the porch, pointing a finger at Hailey.

"It's nothing!" Hailey hollered after her.

It had better be nothing she thought to herself.

Seven

Expectations

"Jesus Christ Hailey," Will said under his breath as he walked down the hall, leaving Hailey standing alone in their bedroom. She stood still, on the verge of tears and pulled her arms up across her chest as if to hug herself. In moments like these, she honestly wondered what was keeping her here. They seemed too different sometimes and when they argued like this, over stupid things, she felt it as deep as her own heart beating in her chest.

Will had picked up another extra class at the college and it just so happened that the first class fell on the same night as their second wedding anniversary. Hailey knew that in the grand scheme of things, it wasn't really that big of a deal and she understood not being able to really take the evening off. She wasn't looking to put any of his students out, she just didn't get why he took the class in the first place. To Will, it was obvious. It meant he took home a bigger salary and it put him in a better position once the department head came up again. In his eyes, the money and the idea of running the department was important and maybe to most it would be. Hailey just didn't see it that way though and felt that he was prioritizing money and his career over their relationship. They didn't get to spend much time together as it was, with him having an almost hour-long commute one way each day, it turned his normal eight hour working day into ten hours away from home and away from Hailey. Even though this class was only one night a week, it would just add on making for an even longer day. The current department head wasn't looking like he was going anywhere any time soon and the money was nice but it wasn't making or breaking them. Hailey could do without it and had for a long time. Money never mattered much to her as long as she had enough to cover the bills and a little savings; her writing brought in enough to cover any of the extra things they wanted.

She didn't even mean to bring it up and kicked herself as soon as the words slipped out. After all, he had already taken on the class but as their anniversary approached she found herself unable to give a solid performance of being unfazed by the whole situation. She usually did her best to bite her tongue with things like this, but sometimes she let it slip that she felt he was being thoughtless where she was concerned. Like her opinion didn't matter.

She collected herself, stopping in front of her mirror to wipe the dampness from her eyes and take a deep breath before walking to the kitchen, grabbing her jacket and heading outside to the barn. It was early October and although it was still the middle of the afternoon, the fall air felt warmer than it should. Somehow everything just felt off lately and she didn't know what to do about it.

She walked out to the field where she kept Charlie, unsure of what her next move was. She was greeted by a soft nuzzling and without a second thought, she opened the gate and grabbed Charlie's halter and lead rope, slipping it on her before climbing up the fence rail and swinging herself onto Charlie's back. She leaned forward with the rope and tied it to the other side of Charlie's halter, turning it into makeshift reins and headed out for a ride. She needed the quiet of the woods and the strength of her horse to get her wits about her again.

She wasn't the best bareback rider but could manage. She just kept Charlie at a walk and when the path came to a clearing, she closed her eyes for a few seconds, letting herself feel every move Charlie made and hear every sound the world had to offer at that moment. Out here, she didn't have to bite her tongue or hold back her feelings. She assumed Will was still just sitting in front of the tv, shutting out the opportunity to think about their argument or even attempt to see where Hailey was coming from. If she had any real complaints about their marriage, that was a big one. They could never just hash something out in one sitting and getting Will to see things from her perspective was never an easy task. Not that she felt she was always right, but she wanted to feel, at the very least, that he was willing to hear her and try to understand her. Their fights were less frequent than they used to be, but when they did happen, they were just as bad as they ever were. If not worse. They would yell and slam doors or walk away like they did today and although Hailey felt like the argument and its solution was all she could think about for days, Will would go on about his day to day, pretending nothing was wrong, all while giving her the silent treatment. They were both stubborn, but Hailey felt like Will's need to get his way or have the final say didn't work well with her need to actually solve the problem. She wasn't asking for him to change what he had done or how he felt about it. What was done was done. She simply wanted him to calm down long enough to maybe acknowledge that she felt differently about it and should be allowed to and that maybe, he should consider her in situations like these before making final decisions. She wanted him to treat her more like a partner than an afterthought. After all this time together and the connection she thought they had, she felt like he wasn't supposed to see her as that shy, inexperienced 'new' girl that she was when they first met. He was the one who was supposed to really see her, the one who was supposed to understand her. Instead, they would quietly go about the next few days until in the end, they just missed each other and would find some common ground to talk again. Hailey had a feeling that this issue wouldn't be discussed and she would just have to deal silently with her frustration that Will would now be gone more than he already was. She was terrified that they were drifting apart, even though she didn't think things had exactly changed between them, but rather maybe she was what had changed; after all, she was young when they had met and had essentially grown into herself during their relationship. Maybe she just needed more than she used to or at least knew enough now to want more for herself. It was thoughts like this that made her come face to face with the idea that she was feeling so drawn to another man and why over the course of the summer, she had to stifle those thoughts as best she could; otherwise, she was worried it was far too possible for her to be completely consumed by them. Had she changed so much that Will didn't fit her world any longer or that she didn't fit his? Feeling like she didn't have the strength to wander down that rabbit hole, she pushed the thought to the back of her mind and settled on the idea that it was just a fight and things would pass. She headed back toward the house with Charlie and resigned herself to a quiet evening of working away in her office and heading to bed early while Will occupied the living room, had a few drinks and made his way to bed a few hours after her.

Their anger lasted about a week, just long enough for Will to teach the new late night class and Hailey hoped; to feel the wrath of her not waiting up for him the night of their anniversary. She didn't like acting petty, but sometimes, just like her accidental mention of being upset with him in the first place, she let it slip.

She heard him come in that night but stayed in bed. She listened in the dark to him rummage through the kitchen for something to eat. Hailey wished at that moment that she had put her feelings aside and had made something nice for them to eat together on their anniversary, regardless of how late it was or how angry

she had been with him over this whole ordeal. Instead,
she stayed silent in their room wondering if Will would
come in and see if she was awake. It took about an hour
before she heard his footsteps coming towards their room
and as his hand began to turn the knob on the bedroom
door, she closed her eyes and pretended to be asleep. Will
came in quietly, undressed and slipped into bed, facing
the opposite direction and fell asleep quickly. Hailey laid
in bed that night, awake and feeling very alone for what
felt like hours. Her anger seemed to creep back over her
and without hesitation, she sought out the escape of
thinking of Jamie to put herself at ease enough to fall
asleep.

Eight

Like You Were Mine

Hailey always loved Christmas on the farm and when the weather had decided not to cooperate in giving them any snow all throughout November and into the beginning of December, Hailey had thought her white Christmas wouldn't arrive. She held off on decorating anything for the longest time, not that she was one of those people to have the Christmas decorations up the day after Halloween, but the month before Christmas always seemed like the right timing for her. This year she put it off even further, waiting until almost the second week of December. Without any signs of snow, it just put a bit of a downer on her holiday cheer.

When she finally decided not to wait any longer, she dug the boxes of decorations out of the attic and turned her living room into Christmas central. Indoor garland in one pile, outdoor garland in another and then there were the boxes of tree, house and barn decorations. She didn't overdo it, but she liked to spread the classic holiday look over the whole farm, barn included.

She moved the barn boxes to the door and pulled on her boots and coat, picked up the boxes and headed outside to get to work. Once in the barn, she opened the boxes to find the stall door bows and put them up first. She only ever used one stall, but for consistency's sake, she put a red bow on all six stalls. She grabbed the ladder and two big wreaths and headed out to the front of the barn. The wreaths hung on either side of the barn doors every year, but she needed a ladder to get them up on the hooks. She put one of the wreaths over her arm and climbed up on the ladder; just as she reached the top she heard a truck coming up the lane. Curious as to who was popping by since she hadn't been expecting anyone, she turned to look and was surprised to see Jamie pulling up with his trailer hooked up. He stopped out front of the barn and got out.

"Doing a little decorating?" he asked.

"Yea. Well, I put it off for a bit too long this year. Thought I'd better get on it. What are you doing here?"

"Well Merry Christmas to you too darlin'!" he said, putting his hand up to his chest like he was in pain and shooting her a look of hurt feelings.

Embarrassment at how rude she sounded, she apologized. "I'm sorry. I didn't mean it like that. Did I get my dates wrong? I thought you weren't here until next week."

He walked over to the base of the ladder and pulled out his phone. "Hmmm, well that depends. What day do you think it is? Cause I have you booked in for today."

"Shit, I'm sorry. Hang on, I'll go get Charlie."

She placed the wreath on the hook and took a few steps down the ladder but lost her footing and started to fall backwards. Jamie reached up and caught her just before she fell off completely. His hands holding her securely by the waist as her hips leaned against his chest, her hands landing on his shoulders to brace herself.

"You should probably lay off the eggnog if you're going to climb ladders," he joked.

"You're a funny guy!"

He lifted her off the ladder and set her down on the ground. Looking shyly into his eyes, while his hands still lingered on her waist, she quietly said "thank you." No sooner had the words come from her mouth, than a tiny cold snowflake landed on her nose. She looked up to the sky, her hands still on his shoulders, to see the snow beginning to fall. Her eyes lit up and a huge smile made its way across her face. "There it is," she whispered quietly.

Jamie found himself watching Hailey instead of the snow and realized he was still holding onto her. He knew he had absolutely no good excuse for it, but he allowed his hands to stay where they were for a moment longer before letting her go. As he slipped them from her waist, she looked away from the snow and back to Jamie. She let go of his shoulders and with a shy smile, said, "I'll be right back with Charlie."

While she was out in the field, Jamie moved the ladder and put up the second wreath that she had laid against the barn, waiting its turn. It had been months since he had had the chance to be that close to her and without making the conscious decision, he replayed the moment in his mind, essentially committing to memory every tiny detail, right down to the way her hair smelled and how she lit up when she saw the snow. It had begun to come down a little heavier while he waited for her and by the time Hailey had made it back to the barn, a thin dusting already covered the ground. She immediately noticed that the second wreath had been put up and it made her smile that he would go out of his way to do that for her.

"Here she is!" she said as she walked Charlie into the barn, putting her in the crossties. "Thanks for waiting and for putting up that wreath. I probably would have killed myself trying to do it later."

"Well we can't have that now, can we."

They chatted away while Jamie worked, talking about each other's holiday plans and telling funny stories about past Christmas'. Over the last year, Hailey had lost her nervousness about saying the wrong thing around him and had begun to feel like he was someone she could be relaxed and comfortable around. Her only hesitation with him was that she worried he would catch on to how much she had begun to like him.

"Well, she's all done," he said. "I guess I'll see you next year!"

"Good one!" She laughed. "I guess you will! Thank you. And sorry again for mixing up my days."

Jamie started taking his tools out to his trailer and suddenly Hailey remembered that she had forgotten more than just their appointment. "Oh shit! Jamie..." she called out after him. "I have something for you. Well, I will have something for you, for Christmas. It's just not ready yet since I managed to mess up the date you were coming."

"You don't have to do that," his voice sounding grateful that she even thought of it.

"Well I do; I want to. Think of it as a Christmas bonus, and now that you've saved me from certain death by ladder, I will have to add to it. I'll text you early next week to find out where you're working and maybe I can bring it out to you. I hope you have a sweet tooth."

"Alright, sounds good, thank you," he said and jumped in his truck and drove away, waving out the window before he disappeared out of sight.

Hailey stepped back inside the barn and picked up a brush to groom Charlie. It was something she had always found relaxing and allowed her to let her mind drift. Usually, she found herself lost in new ideas for whichever book she was working on at the moment, but this time she had something else on her mind. She found herself staring at the door of the barn as she mindlessly moved the brush back and forth across Charlie's side, picturing Jamie still standing there and imagining every move he had made. But in her daydreaming state, she allowed herself to conjure up moments that hadn't happened. Somehow, there seemed to be a real closeness between them, and her mind wandered with that idea. Imagining a longing look and inevitably a touch that she knew was wrong. She envisioned him walking towards her…

"Do you want a beer? You're my last stop of the day and I just so happen to have a case in the truck," he said as he glanced back toward the barn door, pointing to his trailer.

With a coy smile, she nodded. "I'd love one."

Jamie stepped out toward the truck and grabbed two beers from the case in the back as Hailey followed him out. He handed her one of the bottles and said "Pull up some tailgate," before sitting down and gesturing for her to sit next to him on the back of his trailer.

"Is your husband home?" he asked nervously.

"No, he won't be home until after six tonight. Very rarely is he ever home before then."

"Ah, ok. Didn't want to get you in any trouble if he was. Probably wouldn't look the best if he saw you sitting here with me having a drink."

"I honestly don't think he'd even notice at this point"

"What do you mean?"

"He doesn't seem to notice much where I'm concerned these days."

"I have a hard time believing that"

"How so?"

"I mean, I'd notice you." He paused for a mere moment. "I do notice you."

Looking at him with wonder in her eyes, she smiled as she asked, "You notice me?"

"Of course I do. Who wouldn't!"

She was unable to take her eyes off his. Something was clearly building and although she knew it was wrong, she couldn't help but beg to see where it would go.

Conjuring up a moment of boldness, she took a deep breath and asked, "What do you notice about me?"

"I notice that you're a major pain in my ass when you want to book a trim. I also notice that you have about the prettiest eyes I've ever seen. Your ass ain't bad either," he said with a nervous smile.

"Jamie!" she said, laughing and giving him a little nudge with her shoulder.

"Did I just make things real awkward between us?" he asked.

Smiling coyly again, her eyes still locked on his, she said "No."

"What if I told you that if you keep looking at me like that, I'd be tempted to kiss you?"

Her heart began to pound in her chest with anticipation that he just might lean in and allow his lips to touch hers. "Do you want to?"

"Yea…I kinda do."

"Are you going to?"

With that, his hand reached up toward her cheek, and she leaned into his palm with a certain surrender. He moved closer, turning slightly toward her and let his lips ever so gently graze hers. A touch that was seeded with tension and fear but was a gateway to something she had longed for since the day they met. One graze was all either needed for permission to get completely and utterly lost in a passionate kiss.

Charlie stomped her foot and Hailey snapped back into reality. She took a deep breath and looked away from the door and back to her horse who had been waiting patiently while she was lost in a day dream that left her feeling shaky and guilty. Running her hands along

Charlie's neck she whispered, "I'm getting myself into trouble aren't I?"

Hailey had finished all her decorating by the weekend and had even managed to go out with Will to cut a Christmas tree at the local tree farm. She had never had a fake tree in her life so cutting her own was always really important to her. She had spent all day Sunday baking up a storm, having Will taste test holiday treats until he begged her to stop. Yes, she needed to make sure everything tasted the way it should, but she also used the task as a way to lessen her guilty mind. If she over indulged Will, just maybe it would subconsciously balance out her daydreaming escapade from the other day in the barn. She put together little tins of goodies for a few friends in town and some of Will's coworkers at the college, labelled them all and put them in their cold storage room to wait until she could deliver them. Then she made up one large box of baking and placed it with the others, conveniently leaving a label off of it. She knew the oversized tin she had made for Jamie might raise a question with Will so leaving it without a name was the best idea. Closing the door, she took a deep breath and walked toward the couch where Will was sitting and curled up next to him in front of the tree to soak up a quiet night together in front of the lights.

On the Monday morning before Christmas, Hailey gathered up all the boxes of baking for Will's coworkers for him to take in. Normally she brought the gifts to his work Christmas party, but she hadn't decided if she was even going to go this year, not that she had told him that. She simply said it was probably easier on everyone to not have to worry about another thing the night of the party and thought it best if he just delivered them at work during the day. After Will had left for work, she packed up the rest of the boxes to deliver to their friends in town and grabbed her phone and sent Jamie a quick text.

"Hey, I'm heading into town this morning and happen to have your Christmas gift with me. Any place I can meet up with you? It's kind of refrigerator sensitive. Unless you're really hungry this morning ;)"

Knowing he wouldn't get back to her for a while, she took everything out to her truck and locked up the house. She was nearly finished with her drop-offs when her phone finally buzzed.

"Not in town today. I'll text you if I'm in the area later this week."

His message left her feeling confused. One day he's doing things like helping her put wreaths up, the next he's vague and lacking in any sort of personal tone. Maybe he just felt uncomfortable accepting something from her and was trying to put it off? She wasn't sure but didn't want to push her luck.

"Okay," she wrote back, even though she really wanted to ask him what was with the mood swings.

Jamie felt bad for essentially blowing Hailey off about the Christmas present. He knew she had gone out of her way for him, something she didn't have to do and he hated that she might think badly of him for reacting the way he did. He had taken the day off work, at the request of his wife, to get some Christmas shopping done and she had seen the gist of the text Hailey had sent. When she grilled him over why some girl wanted to meet up with him to give him a gift, he dumbed down the situation or at least his part in actually wanting to meet up to receive it and just said a random client had forgotten his Christmas bonus during an appointment and wanted to bring it to him. He said it didn't really matter and not to worry about it.

The next few days went by and he couldn't bring himself to touch base with Hailey in case his wife checked in about the whole thing. After all, he had already said he didn't care about the gift, it would look a little suspicious if he backtracked and went out of his way to go get it.

By Thursday night Hailey realized that Jamie wasn't going to text her and with Christmas on Sunday, she wouldn't see him beforehand to give him his gift. Will was teaching his late class and wouldn't be home until closer to nine that night so she went to the fridge, grabbed a cold beer and on her way to the living room, she stopped in the cold storage room and picked up the box of baking that was meant for Jamie. Annoyed by the whiplash behaviour and more upset than she should have been at the thought that her daydream would always be just that, she took the box to the living room, unwrapped the ribbon that held it together and turned on the tv. She was just about in a chocolate coma and was five beers in by the time Will came home.

"Having a little Christmas party are you?" he joked.

She smirked at him and mumbled, "A girl's gotta do what a girls gotta do."

"Mind if I join you?"

"Sure, but you gotta grab your own baking. This box has seen better days," she said, pointing toward the kitchen where she had left all the extras she had made for them to enjoy at home. Besides, she didn't like the idea of

Will eating food she had made for Jamie. Her thoughts began to race in an attempt to figure out what she was doing with all of this, but she had too much to drink to sort it all out rationally. She sat with Will for an hour and finished off the last of the treats and one more beer, before she made her way to bed. She knew she was brutally attracted to Jamie and loved the little, almost innocent flirting between them that she hoped wasn't just a product of her overactive imagination, but more and more she found herself thinking of him when she was just going about her normal day to day. She just couldn't wrap her mind around what was going through his head either. He spent the entire summer showing up to the farmers market to buy eggs, helping her in the rain and chasing her around with water guns, catching her when she nearly fell off the ladder and it's not like she didn't notice him holding onto her a little longer than was really necessary. Yet he would put off trims and getting paid, missing their appointments for sometimes a week and his messages back were more often than not, short and lacking in any sort of personal way. After all, they had now known each other for over a year and she figured that at this point, things should be a little less business and a little more acquaintance. He was a mystery to her but maybe that's why she was so interested.

The following night was Will's work holiday party and this year the committee that put the event on had decided to step it up a notch. The event was held in the school's auditorium and in past years it resembled a class reunion of sorts. Nothing to fancy, just lots of drinks, food and Santa hats being worn. This year they decided to create an event worth remembering and requested everyone arrive in formal attire. Hailey had woken up that morning feeling a little hungover, unsure if it was the beer or the quantity of baked goods she had consumed the night before. Will had to work but had tossed his suit in his car and asked Hailey to meet him in his office before the party. She hated driving in the city and since she didn't feel well already, toyed with the idea of calling him and telling him she was going to skip the event. After mulling it over more times than she really cared to admit, she decided she had already bought a dress and figured she hadn't actually been out in a while, let alone had any sort of date with Will for a long time so she took a deep breath and began to get ready. She ran a bath and tried to relax first, hoping it would help settle her uneasy feeling. Once she was done, she wrapped herself in a towel, rubbed a vanilla scented moisturizer into her skin and began to do her hair and makeup. She curled her hair and put it up in a simple, but elegant updo and kept her make up natural, aside from the red lipstick she bought special to match the colour of her dress. Although she still wasn't one to think she was anything out of the ordinary, she liked that getting dressed up made her feel like at least Will might take a second look her way when he saw her. With the imagined image of him doing a double take, she began to feel bold and excited. The idea that maybe he would be more interested in getting her back home again than staying at the party made her change her mind about the underwear she had laid out with her dress. She walked back to her dresser, opened the drawer and tossed them back in, pulling out a pair that were a little more enticing and slipped them on. She wasn't much for jewelry, adding a small pair of fake diamond stud earrings she had bought years ago to her

look. The deep red lace dress and black heels were the
final touches and once she had them on, she smiled at
the thought of Will desperately wanting to get them back
off of her.

Hailey arrived at Will's office just after five o'clock.
She took a deep breath and ran her hands down her waist
and over the poofy skirt, making sure her dress was
where it should be. She adjusted the off the shoulder cap
sleeves and paused a moment to take note of the doors
nameplate; "Professor Will Jenkins". This was his other
world, a world she didn't have much part of and in a way,
it made her sad that she had only stood in front of this
door a handful of times and out of those times, she had
failed to actually admire the importance of it all. She
finally knocked on the door and waited to hear his voice.

"Ya, come on in," he hollered.

Hailey turned the handle on the door and opened it
cautiously as she stepped inside.

"Oh, I'm sorry. I thought you wanted me to meet
you here at five?" she questioned after seeing that Will
was all dressed for the party and having a drink with a
colleague.

"Hailey, come in. It's fine," he said, gesturing to her
to close the door and have a seat.

"Mike, this is my wife Hailey. Hailey, this is Mike.
He's the new guy I was telling you about." Will patted
Mike on the shoulder with a laugh like it was an ongoing
tease to be the new guy.

"Nice to meet you Mike," she said. "I trust my
husband isn't hazing you too much."

"Nah, he's been a great guy to have around these last few months. Getting to know my way around campus and get settled into the job."

Hailey stood in the middle of the office feeling less than comfortable, realizing she didn't know how to navigate this world. It wasn't hers and it startled her to know that Will never considered that. He hadn't done a double take, he hadn't even stood to greet her from where he was sitting on the edge of the desk.

"I suppose it's about time we head over, they'll be serving dinner soon," Will said as he reached for his suit jacket, slipped it on and grabbed his keys to lock up.

Dinner proved no different with Will laughing it up and enjoying the evening with his friends and colleagues, leaving Hailey feeling as an outsider and like she truly didn't fit in. When dinner was cleared, the tables were moved and the room opened up into what looked like a winter prom. Christmas trees with off white lights scattered around lit the room beautifully. Hailey watched Will from a few steps away, thinking about all the ideas she had before arriving of how the night would go and how it had been so far from what she had envisioned. She was on the verge of tears and was about to excuse herself to find a washroom when it dawned on her that Will probably wouldn't notice if she disappeared for a bit anyway.

Without saying a word, she wandered off into the halls, paying close attention as to not get herself lost and found her way back to Will's office. He had locked the door but during dinner had asked her to keep his keys in her clutch. Remembering she had them, she dug them out and unlocked his office, stepping inside and closing

the door behind her. Turning the main light on, she
walked toward his desk, grazing her fingertips across the
dark walnut edge. Turning, she noticed the art he had
carefully chosen to hang on the walls. All modern, all
masculine and not a single image of her. Not a wedding
photo or any sort of reminder of her existed in this room.
A room he spent more hours in than he did his own
home. Hailey's heart sank and she reached for the back
of Will's desk chair for balance. How did they end up
here? Her mind racing, wondering if this is how it had
always been, maybe she just hadn't noticed.

Her phone buzzed in her clutch.

"Where did you wander off to?" Will wrote.

Hailey took a deep breath, stood up straight and
texted him back. *"Just to a washroom. I'll be right there."*

She put her phone away and took the keys back
out of her purse, turned off the light and stepped back
into the hall, locking the door behind her.

When Hailey entered the auditorium, she took a
deep breath and scanned the room for Will. Finding him
not far from the door, she walked toward him and smiled
as she approached.

"Sorry I was gone for so long, I got caught up in the
history of the building. It's impressive." She wondered if
maybe she simply hadn't allowed herself to be a part of
his world, had never tried to be and maybe that was the
reason he seemed to not see her tonight. Had she been so
caught up in her own lifes wants and needs that she just
didn't allow herself to be a part of his as well?

For the next hour, Hailey stuffed her shyness deep
down inside and slipped her arm in Wills as if to force her
presence and make herself be known. She hung onto

every word he said to colleagues and laughed at all his
jokes. She played the part of the doting Stepford wife to
the point she felt sick to her stomach. And somehow,
even though this was the only thing she could think to do
in order to save face, she thought if Will realized what she
was up to he would feel badly for her instead of thankful
that she tried. It must have seemed odd to him that she
wasn't acting her usual quiet or shy self.

The drive home that night was welcomed. Normally
Hailey would have preferred that they drive together, but
since they both had a vehicle there, she followed him
home and it gave her a chance to think. Will was already
in the house by the time she pulled in the laneway. She
turned the truck off and sat staring at the lights shining
through the kitchen window. It had been a long night and
she knew deep down that the ideas she had of how this
night would end were not in the cards and she knew she
could easily allow herself to be upset by that and put
those feelings on Will, but that would just cause a blow
out she didn't have the energy to fight. So she took a
deep breath and decided to play perfect happy wife for a
few more moments, just long enough to get to bed and
hopefully find a good night's sleep.

By the end of January Hailey had all but convinced
herself she had her head in the clouds where Jamie was
concerned and had been making herself believe there was
something there on his side of things when there wasn't.
If she struggled to be seen by her own husband, how
could she allow herself to think that a man like Jamie
would even acknowledge her existence? He was just a
nice guy who probably treated everyone the exact same
way and she wasn't anything special to him after all. She

felt foolish and embarrassed to have even questioned his motives for being kind to her.   She had slowly begun to go back to normal life where Jamie wasn't crossing her mind for no reason at all and had been working heavily on her writing, a welcome distraction to lose herself in another world where he didn't exist. She was only a few weeks away from being ready to publish her book and had just sat down at her desk preparing to go over some final edits when her phone buzzed. *"You going to be around tomorrow morning?"* the text read.

She hadn't heard from Jamie throughout the holidays and was surprised that he had actually written her in time for a regular trim. She had expected she would have to get a hold of him in the next few weeks to try to arrange something and had been dreading the moment she had to face him. It had been hard enough to swallow the idea that she had created something out of nothing but to have to try and avoid thinking that way the next time she saw him seemed like a task far bigger than she was comfortable taking on.

"I will be. I ate your Christmas present though."
She had sent it before she had a chance to actually think about it and instantly regretted being a little snarky. It wasn't the type of person she ever wanted to be.

"Sorry about that, holidays got busy."
There it was again. The shortness, but not enough to actually have her feeling justified in being upset with him. She was just about to write back when he sent her a second message.

"I'll be there first thing in the morning though. I promise."

'Damn it' she thought. Every single time he did something to upset her, he somehow managed to make her feel like she was overreacting or losing her mind. He had this knack for making sure there was sweet to go with the salt. For a reason she just couldn't figure out, she always forgave him before she could ever decide to. Or at the very least let go of whatever frustration she had about him.

"Thanks, I'll be here."

And in a moment of boldness, just to try and hold her ground a little, she tossed a second text back to him.

"Text me when you're on your way though. I have some work to do around here tomorrow and don't have the time to wait around."

It felt more boss girl in her head as she typed and hit send, although reading it back to herself she realized he probably wouldn't even notice, but it would have to do.

The following morning Hailey busied herself around the farm knowing that first thing in the morning probably wouldn't actually mean first thing in the morning. Will left for work and she poured herself another cup of hot coffee. The weather had gone past it's beautiful December and Christmas snowy feel to January muck and Hailey was just ready for spring already, minus the mud. Bundling up every time she had to head outside to the barn was becoming a pain and she longed for simply slipping on her cowboy boots and heading out in a tee shirt and jeans.

She had music on in the house and was getting ready to throw a load of laundry on when she heard a knock at the door. She grabbed her phone from her pocket on her way to answer it, checking her messages to see if Jamie had texted. No text so she was surprised to see him standing on her front porch when she opened the door.

"I know, I suck. I forgot to text you," he said. "But hopefully I can make up for it with coffee?" He shrugged his shoulders up in a way that said 'forgive me?' with a hot coffee in each hand.

"You're really not so good at that whole communication thing you know." She grabbed her jacket and slipped it on.

"I know. I don't get a lot of time to get back to people and even when I do, I'm usually driving and trying to use the speech to text thing. Doesn't always go so well." He handed her a coffee and hoped that was believable. For the most part, it was true but it wasn't exactly why he was being so short and silent with her lately. He had absolutely no way of saying that he was afraid his wife would catch onto how he had been feeling about her without accidentally telling her he was falling for her.

Hailey put her boots on, allowing herself to buy into that idea and let her mind accept that as a good enough reason for the short and non-friendly texts she usually received from him. She knew it was an excuse, but given how sincere he sounded, she almost forgot how irritating it was. She led the way to the barn, having already brought Charlie in for breakfast and put her in the crossties for him.

Picking up Charlie's leg, he said "Listen, I really am sorry I didn't get back to you over the holidays. I really appreciate you going to all that work though."

Did he actually feel bad or did he just notice she was annoyed and was trying to suck up to her?

"Well..." she said, "it really was too bad. That was some damn good baking. Went down well with a few beers too!"

She felt hell-bent on making sure he realized he should show her a little more respect or at the very least, consider her. She didn't want to be a doormat client, she had too much of that type of thing in her marriage already and so she felt like she needed to stand up to him. Maybe if she had stood up to Will in the beginning when he ignored where she should have some input, he wouldn't make big decisions without her now. Maybe he would take her more seriously.

"Oh, it did eh? Now I'm really sorry I missed out."

The fact that he wasn't avoiding the conversation had her struggling to keep her guard up. She wasn't used to having someone willing to hash out a problem with her, let alone apologize.

"Play your cards right cowboy and you just might have something to take home next time." She knew how she meant it, but realized it didn't so much sound that way coming out of her mouth and she felt her face instantly go flush.

He laughed and said, "alright, that sounds like a deal." He couldn't help but let the idea of taking her home instead of a box of baked goods creep into his mind. He knew what she meant, but he also knew that by how quickly she had started blushing that she had also realized it could be taken another way. It wasn't the first time she had made a slip like that with him and he found it cute when she realized it and acted nervous or embarrassed by it.

Nine

When It Rains It Pours

The snow and cold weather had lingered on well into the middle of April; melting, only to reappear just when it seemed the grass might actually start to grow, making for a very long winter. It made sense though since it started late, why wouldn't it run late, or at least that was Hailey's way of making sense of how irritating it was. They were finally starting to see some warmth and she was thankful for the sun since it was beginning to dry up some of the mud. It was a good day the morning she looked at the fourteen-day forecast and realized she could finally put her winter coat away for the year and that by the look of things, she wouldn't need a jacket at all by the end of the month.

When her phone buzzed in the back pocket of her jeans, she pulled it out to check her message and smiled when she saw it was Jamie. He was writing to book Charlie's trim at the end of the following week and wondered if that Friday around noon would work.

"What are you smiling about?" Will called from the living room where he could see Hailey standing in the hall towards the bedroom.

"Huh? Oh, Just Amanda. She's in wedding mode again." She lied. She didn't want to and to be honest, she didn't even think about it before she did it. It was a simple text from her farrier, it's not like Will didn't know she had a farrier. The problem was, she didn't have a reason to have a great big grin on her face.

"When is she not? Good luck with that." Will laughed as he accepted her story and turned his attention back to the news.

Hailey turned her phone off and put it back in her pocket. She headed the rest of the way down the hall to their bedroom and closed the door slightly, walked over to the bed, pulled out her phone again and sat down. She realized she had let the idea of Jamie creep into her mind again, but tried to at least keep the idea that he somehow felt something similar at bay. At the very least, it allowed her guilt to dissipate a bit; lots of people openly have crushes on movie stars or acknowledge attractive people in passing to their spouses. Just because she never had, nor would she admit this to Will, it wasn't so bad if she secretly found some kind of attraction to Jamie. It wasn't hurting anyone or anything if the feelings weren't reciprocated and acted on. At least this was the idea she was going with at the moment so she didn't feel crushed under the pressure of being a perfect wife when she knew damn well she wasn't. Opening her messages, she clicked on Jamie's name to write him back that Friday at noon worked perfectly. Then realizing that Will was leaving that morning for a weekend teaching lecture, she found herself writing back again asking if he had any interest in a trail ride after. She had over a hundred acres of farm fields and wooded trails and was always alone when she went out on them. She told herself it would just be nice to have someone to come along that liked that sort of thing but she knew deep down she was actually just interested in finding a way to spend some more time with him. Suddenly she panicked thinking she just made a fool of herself. It was the bloody Christmas gift situation all over again. She puts out something weird and uncomfortable and then he ignores her in an attempt to avoid the situation. Why on earth would he want to go on a trail ride with her?! For all of the time they had known each other, not once had they actually spent any time together outside of their appointments or farmers market run-ins and even then, he never stuck around longer than it took to complete the job or make a purchase. Everything about their relationship, in reality, screamed work acquaintance. What it did not do, was paint a picture of actual friendship or mutual attraction.

    She dropped her phone on the bed feeling embarrassed and wishing she could take it back. As she was about to pick it up and text him yet again to tell him to forget about it, she forgot she had plans; her phone buzzed.

"Crap," she whispered, realizing she wasn't quick enough to save herself. She picked up the phone and turned it over to read his inevitable decline of her ridiculous offer.

"That would be great actually. I haven't been out for a ride in a while and Joe's been pretty pissy with me about it. I'll have to work out a few things first, but we'll be there for noon."

Dumbfounded she simply wrote back *"okay, sounds great! See you next week."*

Not only had he said yes, but his text wasn't short or vague and it had her smiling a ridiculously large smile!

"Hey babe," Will called from the living room, making Hailey jump. The smile disappeared from her face about as fast as it had gotten there.

"I'm going to make up some lunch." Will's voice was sounding closer and she realized he was coming to the bedroom. She stood up, shoved her phone back in her pocket and walked over to her dresser where she kept a bottle of lotion. Pumping a few drops into her hand and rubbing it in as Will stuck his head in the doorway.

"Anything special in mind?" he asked.

Hailey looked over at him and smiled. "Whatever you want is fine with me. I'll come help though." With the excitement of her texts with Jamie still reeling inside her mind, she felt guilt the second she heard Will's voice and the only thing she could think to do was be as close to him right now as she could in an attempt to make up for it. Making lunch together seemed like a good start.

Jamie made sure to delete the texts with Hailey from his phone on the off chance his wife might accidentally or otherwise bump into them. He didn't really know if Hailey's invitation meant more than just a simple ride together; he had thought a few times that she might have at least a slight interest in him, but with both of them being married, it was hard to tell what was really going on without crossing a line that he couldn't come back from. He didn't want to risk Amy getting upset over something that he didn't even understand himself. He also knew that since he was hiding it from her, he probably shouldn't be going, but he felt compelled to and against his better judgement, he said yes.

Friday morning rolled around and Hailey was up early busying herself around the barn and the house to try and occupy her mind. Will was all packed for the weekend and ready to go by eleven o'clock. He had invited her to go with him when the trip was first booked but she had turned him down. As much as she loved being married and genuinely wished Will's work days weren't always so long, she also really loved her alone time when she knew she wasn't necessarily just waiting around for him to come home; not all the time, but every once in a while. She felt it was good for her creativity to get lost in her work. Will knew it gave her an opportunity to write on her own timeframe and so he was happy to take the trip without her and let her get to it. Besides, he would be spending most of the time away at lectures and Hailey would probably end up spending the time sitting alone in a hotel room.

"Ok, I'm off. I'll give you a shout when I get there. Please make sure your phone is on you in case of any emergencies," he said. "I hate the thought of you getting hurt here when you're alone."

Hailey walked to the door to say goodbye. "I'll be just fine. You don't have to worry about me."

"I know, but I do anyway. You're out here alone and anything can happen. Just be careful and keep your phone on you please."

"I will," she said as she smiled and leaned in to give him a goodbye kiss and hug. "Drive safely please."

"Will do." And with that, Will was out the door and on his way.

Since she had all her barn chores done early, all she had to do was get Charlie from the field and bring her up to the barn. She ran quickly to her bedroom and started digging through her closet. Jamie would be here in less than an hour and she was not exactly company ready. At least not when you are trying for some reason to impress that company. She grabbed the jeans that Will had once said made her ass look amazing and took off the ugly sweatpants she had been wearing all morning. Feeling ridiculously guilty for putting those jeans on she took off the tee shirt she had on which just happened to be Wills and buried it in the laundry hamper. She pulled her blue plaid button up off a hanger and tossed it on, tucking it into her jeans and looped her brown belt into her pants before she walked over to the mirror in her room and took a good look.

"Well, I certainly don't look like I'm just hanging around my house today and riding my horse through my own damn woods. What in the hell am I doing!?" She looked up at the clock. Eleven twenty-five. "Shit. Guess we're going with this." She ripped the elastic out of her hair that had been holding up a messy bun, fluffed and finger combed her long brown hair to give it what she hoped was that messy but hot look. She ran to the bathroom to brush her teeth and put some kind of makeup on. She didn't want to look like she was wearing makeup but put the basics on to at least look like she normally puts in some effort each day. While she was putting on her mascara, she had flashbacks of the first day she had ever spent time with Will outside of work, when they were both still working at the firm. The rush to look effortlessly attractive and the nervousness in the pit of her stomach.   She never fathomed she would be here again.

She walked to the front door and grabbed her boots, sliding her feet in, feeling as ready for this as she figured she could be. The wooden door was open still so she peeked out the screen to make sure Jamie wasn't early. As she grabbed her phone she remembered that she couldn't fit in the back pocket of these jeans since they were so fitted. "Oh well," she said as she put her phone back down on the kitchen counter and out the screen door she went.

She had just brought Charlie into the barn and was putting her in the crossties when she heard the sound of Jamie's truck coming up the lane. In a moment of pure nerves and mindlessness, she popped the top button on her shirt and adjusted her bra. "Jesus woman, what are you doing!?" she said in a low voice but before she could even decide to do the button back up she heard the truck door close and his boots in the gravel walking toward the barn.

"Hey, how are ya?" he shouted as he came into view.

The sound of his voice, deep and a little rough with that accent, took her breath away. The attraction she felt to something as simple as his voice was overwhelming and she struggled to do anything but beg him to just keep talking. Knowing that today was, even if in a lesser way than she secretly hoped, bringing them closer together had every sight and sound hitting every nerve she had. His presence alone had her body on edge and her mind racing with excitement.

"Good! How're you doing?" She felt like it was far too noticeable that she was trying to get his attention but maybe he wouldn't notice. "Women dress like this all the time and I'm sure plenty of his clients do too," she thought to herself.

"We still on for a ride after?" he asked.

"Yea of course, if you still have the time?" She knew she would be crushed if he was hoping to back out of the idea, so giving him an easy out felt like the only way to save herself from looking broken if he changed his mind.

"Sure do, you're my last appointment for the day. I'll just go get Joe out of the trailer and bring him in."

Hailey waited nervously in the barn listening to the sounds outside the door of the trailer opening and Joe stepping backward down the ramp to the ground. She could hear Jamie talking to him and telling him he was a good boy. She took a deep breath and told herself to calm the hell down. Being so concerned about what she was wearing was wrong and she knew Will would be upset to find out she put that much effort in, but it was done already and she couldn't take it back. Gathering up all her strength, she told herself nothing was going to happen that shouldn't so she might as well just go on with things and stop worrying. She quickly reminded herself that it wasn't going to kill anyone for her to enjoy the sights and sounds for the day and that she would figure out how to get her shit together afterwards. Will was away, doing what he enjoyed, why shouldn't she do the same. He had always encouraged her to find a friend to ride with since he had no interest in it. He never said he preferred that friend to be a woman, so technically, she wasn't doing anything wrong.

Joe's nose peeked around the door. As he came fully into view with Jamie by his side, Hailey unhooked Charlie's crossties and said, "I'll turn her around so they can get to know each other a bit."

Once Joe was in the barn and settled, Jamie gave him an apple and headed to the trailer to get his gear, which was a welcome distraction since he was finding it hard not to stare at Hailey. She looked good and his mind was racing trying to come up with something to think about other than wondering what every inch of her felt like.

When he came back in the barn with his tools he quickly asked how Charlie had been, realizing that he needed to get his head in the game and focus on his actual job and the main reason he was there. Once they got chatting, his mind seemed to settle a bit. For as much as he realized he got caught up in just seeing her, he knew he always just as easily got lost in conversation with her.

Hailey craved the way Jamie always hung onto what she was saying. He didn't drift off or interrupt and he always seemed genuinely interested in what she had to say. Will wasn't as easy to talk to and she always felt like it was hard to keep his attention for more than a few sentences or get him to hear her out without changing the subject to something he related to. She knew he didn't really mean anything by it and she tried not to take it personally, but she loved that she had Jamie's full attention when he was with her, it made her feel appreciated.

Charlie's trim was done in no time and Jamie headed out to put his tools in the trailer before coming back in with his tack.

"So what's the trail like?" he asked.

"It's out past the hayfield and goes through the woods and then alongside a creek and back into the woods before looping around to come back. It's pretty easy riding but it's peaceful." She paused for a moment, realizing he hadn't asked for directions. Embarrassed and wondering when she would learn to just relax and speak like a normal human being, she finally finished by saying "It's where I go to think."

"Sounds like a dream. You're lucky to have gotten your hands on this place. It's a beauty."

They got the horses all tacked up and headed out of the barn. Hailey's nerves set in as she realized they weren't farrier and client at the moment. Now they were spending time together as friends, even though she knew damn well she invited him out because she felt more for him than just friendship.

She looked around and realized there wasn't anything for her to stand on to mount and in a moment of now or never she let the words fall from her lips without thinking. "Hey, do you mind giving me a leg up? Short girl problems," she said with a shrug. She knew she could just go in and grab a mounting block but couldn't resist the idea of being a little closer to him.

"Sure thing," he said and he tossed Joe's reins over his head and walked over to Hailey. As he reached for her leg to help lift her up, he caught the smell of her perfume and swallowed hard as if he was pushing his interest in her deep down. He hoisted her up into her saddle, trying not to be overly excited about her needing him, even if it was for something as simple as this.

Hailey wasn't very heavy, 125 pounds at the most, but she couldn't help but notice how easy it was for him. "I guess lifting horse legs all day long has done you well" she laughed.

He gave her a quick smile and looked down at the ground before saying "you aren't exactly very heavy". Then he swung up on Joe and they headed out toward the trail, side by side.

As they were crossing the hayfield Hailey realized it was entirely possible that one of these days, Jamie and Will would actually bump into each other. The thought of Will finding out she went on a ride with Jamie without her having told him first hit her in the pit of her stomach as she realized it wouldn't go over well.

"So, I have a weird request," she said. "Sort of an embarrassing one."

"Okay," Jamie said nervously.

"Can we keep this ride between the two of us? Not that there's anything wrong with this, I just...well, I didn't tell Will we were doing this and now that I think about it, I'm pretty sure he would get the wrong idea. It would just upset him and there's no need to do that. It's weird, I know."

Jamie felt a little like he had been kicked in the chest hearing her say that her husband might get the wrong idea, as if it was out of the question to think this might have been more than just a casual ride. Collecting himself, he gave a quick glimpse of his crooked smile and said, "What's weird is that I was going to ask you the same thing. I didn't tell Amy either."

They looked at each other, both amused by the coincidence and embarrassed that it was even a thing to consider, but both feeling hurt that the other thought nothing more of this ride than something casual. Hailey wondered why he didn't tell his wife what his plans were and why he wanted to make sure she didn't find out. All she knew was she couldn't get this guy out of her head and she wanted to spend time with him and get to know him. Even though, truthfully what she believed was that he had zero interest in her in that way. Maybe that's why she was able to continue being around him. In the end, it's not like anything was going to come of it, but it made her feel alive when he was around so she might as well enjoy it while she could.

They headed out through the back end of the hay field and met up with the path through the first bit of woods. The sun peeked through the trees here and there casting bright streaks of light that made the whole area have a magical feel to it. The air was warm that day and the deeper into the woods they got, they could begin to hear the sound of the water trickling over the rocks in the creek. Hailey hadn't been sure if they would have enough to talk about once they were out there but she found herself not searching for something to say. The change from a working relationship to doing something as friends had her worried that it would make things different. Thankfully it didn't. Conversation between them just came easy. They joked together and laughed, poked fun at each other and even got into some deep conversations about life. There was only one point where neither spoke a word. It was as they were coming to the end of the creek, but instead of the silence feeling awkward, it felt peaceful. It was comfortable being with him and not having to say anything. The path was wide enough that they rode side by side and just took in the beauty of nature. They were about thirty minutes in when they approached the second wooded area and the trail narrowed. Hailey and Charlie took the lead as they entered the trees while Jamie and Joe stayed a few steps behind.

As she rode in, she couldn't help but wonder hopefully if he was looking at her or just taking in his surroundings, the latter being more of what she expected. She wanted so desperately to look back and find out but she couldn't bring herself to do it without a reason. They rode on for a minute or so in silence while she tried to think of something that would give her reason to turn around. Finally she thought, just keep it simple…he's out here, isn't he!? She turned over her right shoulder and looked back at him. He was looking straight ahead at her and smiled when their eyes met.

"Well, what do you think?" she asked, but before he could answer a look of fear fell across his face. "Look out!" he yelled. But it was too late. Charlie reared and although Hailey was a decent rider, she wasn't paying attention and couldn't keep her balance. She was thrown and Charlie took off.

She hit the ground hard on her right side and felt instant searing pain. She closed her eyes tight and just stayed still, waiting for the pain to settle. Jamie was off

Joe in the blink of an eye and ran to her, dropped to his knees and reached for her, holding her still.

"Hailey! Jesus, are you okay?"

She took a deep breath in and opened her eyes. The pain wasn't really going away but she was pretty sure she hadn't broken anything. Maybe just a bad bruise. "Yea I think so. Just...I think I just need a minute. What the hell happened?"

"There was a deer. It bolted across the trail in front of you and Charlie wasn't a fan."

"Where is she?" Hailey said in a panic starting to get up. Then she saw her a ways up the trail. Thankfully she hadn't taken off too far and was happily grazing the tall grass on the side of the trail just up ahead.

As Hailey tried to sit up, Jamie took her left hand in his and put his other hand on her back to help her up. She got to her feet and tried to act like she wasn't as hurt as she felt.

"Shit, you're bleeding pretty good," he said when he saw her back. "Lift up your shirt." The words leaving his lips before even he had the chance to comprehend how there was a good part of him that would be crossing a line by asking her that. She might have been hurt and needed the help, but he knew damn well that he couldn't fully shut off the part of him that had only been growing more and more interested in her since the day he first laid eyes on her.

How in the midst of feeling this kind of pain, she had the ability to let her mind wander here, but he had just asked her to lift her shirt; it left her frozen and not because of the pain. It wasn't exactly how she imagined it happening, but hell, she wasn't going to argue, especially when the moment was, in reality for an entirely different purpose than what her daydreams would have thought up. She grabbed the bottom of her shirt to lift it but as soon as she tried, she dropped her right arm in pain.

"Well this wasn't exactly what I had in mind when I invited you out today," she said with an embarrassed smile.

"It was just an accident. Could have happened to anyone. I've been thrown enough in my life. Here, let me do it."

She turned slowly so her back was to him and he reached down to lift the back of her shirt up, untucking it from her jeans. He was careful not to touch her skin, feeling like it would be the thing that pushed his self-control too far. The wound was just to the right of her shoulder blade which made sense why she couldn't lift her arm without feeling like she was in horrible pain.

"Can you hold this here? With your left hand preferably?" he said, smiling as he said the last part.

She smiled back, glancing over her shoulder. "Good thinkin' with the comedic relief!" As she grabbed for the edge of her shirt, their hands grazed each other and for a brief moment, she didn't feel any pain. Here she was standing in the middle of the woods on a beautiful warm spring day, with a guy she couldn't stop thinking about, her shirt lifted up and him getting up close and personal with her body. How the hell was she going to explain this to Will when he got back?

Hesitating when he realized he couldn't avoid touching her any longer, he moved the back of her bra which was torn up, but not completely ripped, up and out of the way since it was covering some of the damage.

"I just need to wash some of this blood away so I can see what we're dealing with here," he said as he

headed for his trail pack. When he came back, he took
the cap off a bottle of water and poured about half of it on
her shoulder blade, letting it run down her back and side.
He put the cap back on and dropped the bottle on the
ground before putting his left hand on her to hold her
steady.

His hands felt warm and strong. A little rough but
in a good way. She bit her bottom lip and let out a slight
groan as he put a little pressure on her wound with his
other hand. To ease the pain she tried to distract herself
by concentrating on the fact that Jamie was half way to
seeing her naked at this point.

"You got yourself a good gash." He paused. "I think
you're gonna need to get that stitched up."

"Fantastic," she said with a sarcastic tone. "I'm
sorry, clearly, we should be heading back."

"Don't be sorry. It's been an adventure. I need to
stop this from bleeding though before we go or we might
end up with more of a problem on our hands. Do you
have bandages or anything close to it in your pack?"

"Well I do, but funny thing... I didn't bring my
pack."

Jamie looked around to see what he could use.
"Well I don't have anything sterile unfortunately but I do
have my tee shirt." He had started to untuck his plaid
shirt, which just about made Hailey drop to the ground.

"It's just a shirt taken off kinda day today!" she said
with amusement.

"Jamie shook his head and laughed "yea it seems
that way. Although I'm gonna have to take mine off a
little more than you did." He seemed a little shy which
isn't something she would have guessed. He slid the
button up off and dropped it on the ground at his feet. He

took a step behind her, just almost out of view, but not completely and pulled off his white tee shirt.

"So let me get this straight, you get to stand back there changing in privacy, while I have to stand here feeling half naked for all to see?" She said as she glanced over her shoulder. "I highly doubt that's fair!" Suddenly she felt very raw and embarrassed. What possessed her to be that bold was a mystery to her.

He looked down at himself with his tee shirt in his hands and then walked around in front of her. Tossed his arms out to the sides, smiled and said, "there ya go...fair?"

Highly amused and completely unable to hide a huge smile, she laughed and nodded her head in agreement. That was an image she wasn't going to let leave her mind for a very long time to come! He put his arms down and walked back around behind her to figure out how he was going to hold this to her for the ride back.

"I'm going to have to tuck this down behind your..." he paused, feeling uncomfortable talking to her about her bra. "...down here, to get it to stay." Hoping she understood what he was talking about. He tried to pull the elastic out as far as he could to slide the shirt down behind but she pulled away and let out a cry of pain. "Guess I'm going to have to undo it first," he said realizing it would just hurt her too much to do that way.

She felt his hands graze her back softly as he reached for the clasp of her bra and she straightened her back in anticipation. He noticed the small dip in her lower back it created as she moved and couldn't help but imagine the situation without the wound. He reached for the clasp and with both hands undid the hooks. The back of her bra now opened to reveal her entire bare back left her feeling very vulnerable and him feeling beyond drawn to her. He had to stay focused on what he was supposed to be doing vs where his mind was wandering. He folded up his tee shirt to make a thickly padded bandage and placed it against her wound. She took a quick deep breath in as the cloth touched her causing the hurt to begin all over again. Jamie fumbled with the clasp, stretching the bra back over the now bandaged wound in order to hold everything together.

"Not too used to doing these back up, I tell ya," he said.

Hailey smiled nervously and looked slightly over her shoulder at him. She hadn't felt this sense of need in a very long time and it made her feel a sort of grief to know there wasn't anything she could actually do about it. They were both married and she wasn't even sure if Jamie was actually interested in her at all.

He lowered her shirt back down for her and grabbed his button up off the ground, sliding it back on. "I'll grab Charlie," He said as he started to do his buttons up and walked away. Something had changed. The air between them seemed tense and neither one really seemed bright and cheerful like they usually were together.

Hailey walked over to Joe and grabbed his reins. He was such a good boy just standing still the whole time. Jamie had him trained well. She was petting his nose as Jamie and Charlie approached them when all of a sudden she started to feel very weak and faint. Her knees began to buckle and her hand slid down Joe's nose.

"Whoah, I've gotcha," Jamie said as he got there just in time to catch her. "Don't you go passin' out on me."

Jamie scooped her up in his arms to make sure she didn't drop to the ground. She took a few minutes to get her head together and a few deep breaths before telling him she was okay. He lifted her up to Joe's saddle and she grabbed the horn with her good arm, pulling herself up and carefully swinging her leg over. Jamie helped her make sure her feet were in the stirrups before grabbing both Joe's and Charlie's reins and started to walk them out.

When they reached the barn about forty-five minutes later, Jamie tied both horses up to the outside rail, reached up and slid Hailey down off Joe, gently putting her feet on the ground.

"You okay?" he asked, breaking the silence. Neither had said a word the entire walk back.

Hailey nodded and said "yea. I'm good. Thank you for everything you did out there. I guess I owe you a shirt eh?"

"Well, we don't need to worry about that now. I'm gonna put these guys in stalls and then we'll get you to the hospital."

Hailey sighed. "You don't need to do that, I can manage. I'm sure you're probably soon going to be missed at home and you've already done more than you needed to."

"You do realize, you just about passed out back there right? You can't drive yourself anywhere. It's fine." he said.

Jamie untied both horses and led them in the barn while Hailey waited outside. When he came back out, without thinking, he put his hand on her lower back as if it was so natural for him to do and said "where are your

keys? I'd rather not have to park this trailer in the
hospital parking lot."

She nodded her head forward to point in the
direction of the keys. "Kitchen counter just inside the
screen door."

She walked alongside him until they got to her
truck. She waited there while he went in and when he
came back out he had her phone and purse too.

"Might need these," he said as he opened the
passenger door and tossed them inside. He reached out
for Hailey's hand and helped her up in the truck and
pulled her seatbelt across her, buckling her in. He closed
the door and came around to the other side. There was
something very intense and close about the way he was
caring for her and driving her around in her truck. She
didn't know why but it felt right.

They arrived at the hospital and when the nurse
asked Hailey to follow her to a room, she got up and
started to walk until she realized Jamie wasn't following.
She turned back to see him standing there with a look on
his face she hadn't seen before. Like he was worried or
sad.

"You coming?" she called out to him.

"Uh, yea. If you want some company, sure."

The nurse showed Hailey to a hospital bed, laid a
gown out and pulled the curtain closed as she told her the
Doctor would be right in to see her.

Jamie looked at Hailey with his eyes a little wide
and let out a slight chuckle before saying "I guess I should
probably step out for a bit."

"Jamie, you can't just bring a girl to the hospital
with only one working arm and then leave her to fend for
herself. Like hell you'll be stepping out for a bit." She

smiled at him before saying "in all seriousness though, I actually could use your help with this if you don't mind. And don't worry, there's no need for me to ditch the pants, so this is basically nothing you haven't already seen."

She turned to face the bed, leaving Jamie to stand behind her and she unbuttoned her shirt, sliding her left arm out effortlessly, for the most part, and then struggling a bit more to get it off her right side. Jamie's white tee shirt was now pretty soaked in blood and it was probably a good thing they were taking it off now.

"Alright, this is where you come in. Don't be shy, it's coming right off this time." Although she somehow managed to find the courage to say the words, it was the opposite of what she felt. Here she was again feeling at her most vulnerable with a man she should not have feelings for while he undid her bra for the second time that day.

Jamie felt like everything was moving in slow motion. He shouldn't be here and he knew it but wasn't about to walk away now. He reached for Hailey, undoing the hooks and letting his fingers graze across her back, wondering if he should slide the straps over her shoulders or if that would be pushing his luck. He imagined doing it but forced himself to let that be as far as it went.

The bloodsoaked tee shirt had fallen to the floor and he reached down to pick it up before turning away so she could have at least a little privacy to undress the rest of the way and get the hospital gown on.

Hailey felt a different kind of pain when she realized his hands weren't touching her anymore. She hadn't actually experienced feeling anything like this before. It was an ache she couldn't describe.

"All set," she said. "Can you do this up for me?" gesturing to the ties on the back of the gown.

Jamie tossed the tee shirt on the end of the bed and brushed Hailey's long hair over her left shoulder. Once again she straightened her back at his touch and he couldn't help but notice that small dip in her lower back.

"Knock knock," said a man's voice outside the curtain. "Everybody decent?" he said before pulling back the curtain and revealing himself to be the doctor. Feeling an abrupt sense of relief mixed with disappointment, Jamie stepped back.

"So, what happened here?" asked the doctor as he motioned for Hailey to turn around so he could see her back.

"I fell off my horse and landed on some rocks and brush." Suddenly Hailey was vividly aware of the fact that the hospital gown material didn't do much for hiding anything. She reached her left arm up over her chest and held her right arm in an attempt to maintain some sort of dignity where her boobs were concerned.

"Are you the husband?" the doctor asked Jamie.

"Uh, no. No, I'm just a friend," he said, a little startled at the question.

Hailey couldn't help but laugh a little when she looked his way. It seemed funny in the moment, after all, they had both kept this entire day a secret from each of their spouses without actually having a real reason to.

Half an hour later Hailey was all stitched up and heading home again with Jamie. He had helped her to get dressed again and held her hand to get her back in the truck. She was quiet on the drive home, thinking about all the reasons she had to feel guilty about now and at the same time replaying all of the moments from the day that she wished things could have gone further. How would she explain all of this to Will and how would she be able to stop thinking about Jamie and how he had held her, touched her and taken care of her. Or did she even want to? All she did know was that he was about to take her back home again, then he would have to leave and go home to his wife and she didn't want him to.

They drove up the long laneway and parked out front of the house. Jamie turned the ignition off and jumped out to come around and open the passenger door. Hailey reached out to brace herself against the door and although she didn't really need too much support to get out, he grabbed hold of her anyway and helped her down. Hailey looked up and smiled at him. "Thank you again, for everything you did today. You went way above and beyond and are probably going to get yourself in trouble once you finally get home."

He shrugged. "Ah, it's not too late. She probably won't even ask. I work late some nights anyway."

"Won't she wonder why you were working late with Joe along for the ride?"

"Well, yea...but I'll just tell her a client of mine had some great trails and I wanted to try em out. It's sorta the truth right?!" he said smiling. "Speaking of Joe, I'd better go get him loaded up. He's probably wonderin' what in the hell is goin' on."

Hailey walked to the barn with him and watched as he loaded Joe on the trailer and closed the gate.

"You going to be okay until your husband gets home tonight?" he asked.

"Yea, I'll be fine. It's just a scratch," she said coyly. "He's away for the weekend though. Work stuff. But I'll be okay. I suppose I'll probably skip the market on Sunday. It's the first of the season, but I suppose it could be worse."

"Okay well, we'll have to give that trail a try some other time. Might bubble wrap you first, but another time for sure."

Hailey smiled with a mild amount of embarrassment and thanked him again for everything he did. He jumped in his truck and pulled away, waving his hand out the window as he left. She waved back and headed into the barn to say goodnight to Charlie and noticed that Jamie had already tossed her some hay.

She turned off the light and headed for the house. It wasn't much past 8 pm but she was exhausted and headed straight for bed.

When she woke the next morning it was already fully bright outside. Realizing she must have slept in she tried to sit up, forgetting that she had stitches in her back. The sharp pain beside her shoulder blade reminded her to take it slow. She sat on the edge of the bed to collect herself when she heard a vehicle in the driveway. Thinking Will must have come home early she stood up and walked to the front door wearing only one of Will's oversized tee shirts. She opened the door and stepped out on the porch only to see Jamie's truck and him opening the door to get out of it.

"It seems to be becoming a thing where each time I see you, you're wearing less and less clothing," he said with a smirk on his face.

Hailey looked down and then back at Jamie with panic on her face. "Jesus," she said and she turned around and quickly went back inside. "What are you doing here?" She yelled through the screen as she headed through the kitchen on her way to the bedroom.

Jamie walked toward the house and opened the screen door, stepping into the kitchen.

"I was heading out this way for work this morning and thought since your husband isn't around, you might need help with morning chores. Figured I would lend a hand."

Looking around the room, Hailey grabbed a pair of jeans off the floor and wiggled into them using one hand. With no bra on or any real way of doing one up, she dug through her dresser looking for a tank top that might help the situation with a built-in bra and Macgyvered her way into it. She walked back out to the kitchen where Jamie was waiting.

"I'm really sorry, I thought you were Will coming home early."

"It's fine," he said with a laugh. "Really, I mean it was quite the welcome!"

Hailey let out a big huff of air and smiled. "I feel like I'm just destined to be fully embarrassed around you at all times."

"How's the shoulder?" he asked, changing the subject.

"Sore, but I think I'll live. Thanks to this guy who stuck around to help me out. His tee shirt didn't fare as well as I did though. Kinda destroyed it. Once I get out this week, I'll buy you a new one to replace it."

"Ah, no worries about the shirt. I have more at home."

Jamie turned toward the door, stepped out on the porch and held it open for Hailey. They walked toward the barn and Jamie quickly got busy throwing in some hay for Charlie while Hailey made up her grain. They stood in silence watching Charlie eat for a while and it was the first time either felt unsure of what to say. She wasn't positive, but she felt like Jamie kept looking at her. Finally, he broke the silence by asking her if she needed help changing her bandage.

Realizing that she probably did but feeling like saying yes was allowing things to go too far, she told him she was pretty sure she could manage it. Her guilt from the day before was weighing heavily on her.   He looked back to Charlie before asking if she wanted some help in the evening.

"I'll be coming back through here around six tonight and can stop in and give you a hand with things if you want."

She knew she wanted nothing more than to say yes and spend as much time with him as possible but she knew she had to stop this at some point.

"Thank you, but I think I'll be okay."

He nodded quietly and kept looking at Charlie. She couldn't help but feel like she had hurt him. After all, turning down his help was making her hurt throughout every part of her being, like she had just turned him away. He opened Charlie's stall and started to lead her out to the field. Hailey followed alongside, neither of them saying a word.

On the way back to his truck Jamie told Hailey he hoped she would be okay on her own until Will got home the following night and let her know that if she did end up needing help with anything to give him a shout. She thanked him and after an awkward silence told him they were still on for a trail ride once she was all healed up. He jumped in the truck and took off down the lane, the dust flying up behind him. And just before he was out of sight, she saw his hand reach out the window and wave goodbye. She watched until he was gone before heading back in the house, feeling like she just broke her own heart, and realizing she had to try and figure out how she was going to explain this injury to Will.

Ten

Homecoming

It was about 6 pm on Sunday evening before she heard Will coming up the lane. She was nervous to try and explain everything but decided that since nothing had actually happened, there was no reason to try and over explain things. She could try to hide the fact that Jamie had been there to help, but if word got out by anyone who had seen her at the hospital, she would have to explain why she kept it a secret. It was just easier to tell the truth, at least most of it. Will had no way of knowing about the trail ride part so she decided that it was still best to keep that part to herself. As for the rest of it, she would have to try and convince Will that he was glad Jamie was there, otherwise, his tendency to get jealous might have him get carried away and assume things she didn't want him to assume.

"Babe! I'm home!" Will yelled as he came in. The screen door swinging shut behind him. Hailey was sitting in the living room and got up to come meet him at the door. He put his bag on the kitchen table and leaned in for a hug. She tilted to the side and told him he had to be careful, that she had a little accident while he was away.

"What do you mean, you had an accident?" he asked.

"I was out with Charlie Friday morning after you left. She spooked and I fell off and landed on some rocks. I'm okay, just hit my shoulder on them and got cut up. It's honestly not a big deal."

Will gave her that look that meant he knew he shouldn't have left her alone.

"It's fine, really. It was just a dumb mistake. I'm a little sore but I'll be back to good in no time," she said.

"Obviously nothing is broken?" he asked.

"No, not broken. Stitches though." Hailey turned around and let him lift up the back of her shirt. She couldn't help but have flashes of Jamie doing the same thing just two days before tearing through her mind.

"Will, it's all bandaged up. You can't really see anything."

Bandages didn't stop him though, he peeled the tape off the top of the gauze and peered down behind it. "Jesus Hailey! Why didn't you call me!? That's really bad!"

"I didn't want you to worry. I was fine, the Doctor's said so and I knew if I said anything you would cut your trip short and there wasn't any need for you to do that." "Hailey, you have a shoulder full of stitches! Honestly, what if it had been worse? That could have been way worse and you didn't have anyone here to help you."

"Actually…" she tried not to hesitate. "Jamie was actually just getting here for Charlie when we were coming back. He saw the blood and drove me to emergency to get checked out."

He stuck the gauze back where it was and put her shirt back down. She turned back to face him, trying almost harder to convince herself than him that there was nothing weird about the entire situation.

"Well good, but next time you call me when something like this happens! Not that I'm ever actually leaving you alone again." The last part coming out with his notorious sarcastic tone.

"Next time Jamie is here, let me know so I can thank him for getting you to a doctor."

Her insides turned at the thought. There was no way she wanted the two of them in the same room together, let alone talking about something she just lied about! Somehow she had to get the story straight with Jamie just in case.

Hailey and Will spent the rest of the evening catching up over a few beers and snuggles with the dogs. She really had missed him when he was away and was glad he was home again. She knew she loved him very much and she didn't want to do anything to put what they had on the line. She just couldn't shake the idea that she felt like she was two people living in one body. Whatever was going on with her feelings toward Jamie were maybe only one-sided, but there was something about him that she craved deeply. What she had with Will was strong and confident. He was home and she knew she needed to be here with him. Still, she hated herself for thinking that there was a chance that no matter how much they loved each other, it might not be everything she wanted or needed. That there was clearly a part of her that had woken up the day she met Jamie and that was a part of her that didn't fit with Will.

Three Sunday's had come and gone since Hailey's accident and Jamie hadn't shown up at the farmers market. In fact, she hadn't heard from him at all. Charlie wasn't due for a trim for another three weeks and she wondered if he would avoid her until then. She toyed back and forth with why he had been so helpful after her accident, showing up the next morning unannounced to help her out, only to have radio silence right after. If he felt anything for her at all, maybe she did hurt him when she turned down his offer to help. Not that it was the offer itself, but the idea of spending more time together. Every person that passed at that market that wasn't him made her ache inside with sadness. She tried to forget that she felt anything at all for him and she clung desperately to the person she was before she had crossed his path, even though she felt like she was grieving a loss she couldn't explain. Both the loss of the idea of a man that wasn't hers and part of herself that she found freed when he came into her life. She held onto Will and tried to focus on their time together but it was a lot harder to do than she had anticipated and she found herself faulting at every turn.

Eleven

Pickup Trucks

It was getting close to the end of June and Hailey had started summer off on the wrong foot. She hadn't really slept in weeks and found herself lost in her own mind more often than not. She knew Will was beginning to notice but she just didn't know what to say to him. Every time her phone would buzz it was all she could do not to jump to see if it was Jamie. The last week had been the worst because she knew she would need to call him to book Charlie. She felt like all her nerves were on edge but there wasn't a soul she could talk to about it. She woke up one morning hours before Will would need to get up for work. Unable to sleep she grabbed her big knitted sweater off the bedpost and slipped it on over the tee shirt Jamie had caught her in that morning he showed up unannounced. She made a pot of coffee, grabbed a cup and headed to the front porch to watch the sun come up. She settled into the porch swing and sipped away on her coffee, welcoming the warmth against the crisp morning air.

As she sat looking out toward the barn she couldn't help but play back what felt like every moment she had spent with Jamie in that laneway. Each wave and smile, the laughter and what she forced herself to believe was unintentional flirting. Remembering the comfort she felt when he was there and the sound of his voice made her smile softly to herself. She missed him more than she could even find the words to say and it left her feeling lost. He wasn't hers to miss, but no matter how hard she tried, she couldn't stop.

Around the time the sun popped up over the barn, Hailey heard Will's alarm go off. She knew she had a few moments left to herself while he showered and dressed. Eventually, she took a deep breath, soaking up the quiet world around her, got up and headed back inside to pour Will a cup of coffee and see him off to work.

"What are your plans for the day?" He asked as he happily took the hot coffee mug from her hands.

"Oh I don't know, I have some writing to catch up on so that'll probably take up most of the day. Amanda is off to the city to do a wedding cake tasting with Collin so I shouldn't have any interruptions," she said with a slight chuckle. Amanda may have been Hailey's best friend but sometimes she didn't realize she didn't leave much time for Hailey to get actual work done. She loved her dearly but was glad Amanda was getting married and secretly hoped it meant she would have another focus for some of her time.

"Well, it's a good thing I'm off for the day then too. You'll have the whole day to yourself to get caught up. I'm teaching late tonight. I'm covering while Mike's away. I'm not sure if I remembered to tell you that. I should be home around nine."

"Yea you mentioned it a few days ago." This time Hailey managed to bite her tongue about his lack of involving her in any choices he had to make where their time together would be affected.

And with that, Will grabbed his keys and coffee to go and kissed Hailey on the cheek on his way to the door. "See you tonight," he said, the screen door swinging shut behind him.

Hailey stood still in her silent kitchen as if she was preparing herself to accept the loneliness that she felt far too often. She wandered toward her office and took a peek through the open door. Her desk sat ready and waiting for her to get to work but something was stopping her. She needed to shake this mood and come back to life. She decided to grab a shower, get dressed and go for a drive to clear her head. The first step was to turn her phone off and avoid the inevitable panic when it buzzed over a junk email or spam phone call. After her shower she dug through her closet, trying desperately to find something to wear that had no memories of Jamie attached. Moving quickly past the torn plaid shirt she wore the day of her accident that she left in the closet with every intention of trying to mend, she settled on a plain white tee and jeans. She towel dried her hair, tossed on a hint of makeup and grabbed her silent phone and keys. She headed to the barn first to grab Charlie's breakfast and took it down to the field for her before heading to the truck. She had no idea where she was headed but knew she needed a change of scenery. She put the keys in the ignition and rolled the windows down, turned the radio on a little louder than she really needed to and headed out the lane. Left or right, it didn't much matter. She was just in the mood to go where the road led her. Twenty-six minutes and seven and a half songs into her drive down long winding dirt roads and she felt and heard a massive clunk and saw smoke start to pour out from under the hood. Hailey pulled over quickly and shut the truck off, grabbed her phone and jumped out. She lifted the hood as if she knew what she was looking for but in reality, she had absolutely no idea what to do.

"Fuck," she said as she took a step back, looking around realizing she had literally driven herself into the middle of nowhere. At least she had her phone on her. She called Will, knowing he was almost two hours away at this point and probably couldn't leave work. No answer. 'Great!' she thought. Amanda was in the city so there was no point in calling her. She scanned the contacts on her phone and name after name just reinforced the fact that she was probably a little too introverted for her own good and didn't really have anyone in her life that she could call in a situation like this. Either the person was too far away or more of an acquaintance than a friend she could call for help. There was only one name in the list that made her pause. The only name she was trying to clear her mind of. She realized she didn't really have a choice so as if to rip off the bandaid she pressed the button to call beside his name without giving herself time to overthink it. After the fourth ring, she closed her eyes thinking he wasn't going to answer. Another ring went by. She opened her eyes and as she lowered the phone from her ear she heard his voice. "Hello?" There it was, that slight country accent that made her melt every damn time.

"Hi. It's..." she paused as her nerves felt like they were going to tear right out of her body. "It's Hailey."

He was quiet and that terrified her.

"Maybe I shouldn't have called..." she said with her voice trailing off. "I just..."

"No it's okay, I needed to give you a shout this week for Charlie anyway," he interrupted.

"Yea, but I actually, well... I didn't know who else to call. Will's at work and I can't get a hold of him and Amanda's in the city and I didn't want to bug you, I just didn't.." she rambled on, clearly nervous to have called him.

"What's going on Hailey? You can always call me. You know that." Suddenly the tone of his voice sounded the way she remembered. Warm and comforting.

"My truck just decided to conk out on me and I'm stuck on the side of the road. I know you are probably nowhere near here and I don't want to bug you or put you out, I just didn't know who else to call."

He was silent for what felt like an eternity.

Hailey put her hand on her forehead and began to pace. "Listen, I can figure this out. I shouldn't have.."

"Where are you? I'm coming to get you." he interrupted.

"Are you sure? I'm out on Fletcher Road."

"Ya, I know the area. I'll be there in about forty minutes. Just sit tight," he said before hanging up. Forty minutes on the dot and she saw his truck coming down

the dirt road. He pulled in behind her and opened the
door to get out. She was nervous and wasn't sure what to
say or how to act. Laying eyes on him for the first time in
over a month she felt like the wind had been knocked out
of her. Struggling to catch her breath as he walked
toward her she managed a quiet "thank you", just loud
enough for him to hear.   He smiled at her and asked how
her shoulder was.

"It's good, thanks."

"That was a pretty good gash," he said as he walked
around to the front of her truck and started to take a look
under the hood.

"Uh, Will wanted to thank you." The moment had
presented itself and she had to make sure her story of
that day was the only story. Plus it gave her a chance to
do Will's job for him and thank Jamie, hopefully avoiding
a face to face collision between the two men.

Jamie looked up from the engine as if he was
caught off guard.

"I didn't tell him we were out on a ride together. I
just said you were at the barn for Charlie's trim when I
got myself back...after I fell. I told him you drove me to
the hospital and dropped me back off at home after."

He looked back to the engine, fiddled with a few
things before standing up straight. "You're going to need
to have it towed." He pulled his phone out of his pocket
and made a call. "Tow truck should be here soon," he
said as he hung up.

"I'm sorry, I should have just called them in the
first place. I guess I panicked and I just wasn't thinking."
She was embarrassed that she had called him and
realized she wasn't sure why she had aside from not really
ever having had to handle this sort of thing on her own.

She knew he wasn't going to fix her truck on the side of the road and he wasn't hers to call on when things went wrong. "You don't have to wait. I'm sure you are really busy."

"It's okay, I already pushed my day ahead to tomorrow. Might as well drop you off and trim Charlie before I go."

She looked at him, her head full of curiosity about what he was thinking. Wishing she could read his mind, she decided she should just make small talk and try to lighten the tension that she wasn't sure he was even feeling. She knew she was though and she needed to say something to lighten the mood. So, of course, she asked him how work was going, saying he must have been really busy lately since she hadn't seen him around. In true Hailey fashion, she felt like she put her foot right in her mouth. When trying to avoid talking about why he hadn't been around, ask him about why he hadn't been around. Small talk was not her strong point.

Saved by the sound of the tow truck, she mumbled "ah, finally" and opened the driver side door to grab the keys, taking the truck key off to give to the mechanic.

They waited while the truck got loaded and pulled away.

"Come on. Let's get you home," he said as he walked around to the passenger side of his truck, opening the door for her.

She smiled nervously as she climbed inside. He shut the door and came around to get in.

"So you said before you knew the area. Do you have clients out here?" she asked, trying to make conversation that didn't end up with her saying the wrong thing.

"Uh, no, I have an old cabin out this way. Just a few miles up the road. Haven't been out here much in the last few years though." His voice trailed off and he seemed to let his mind go elsewhere. His usual chatty self had disappeared. Something had changed and she felt like it was her fault. Maybe asking him for help was too much. She sat quietly, fighting back the tears she felt welling up in her eyes, watching the countryside go by out her window.

After five minutes of dead silence, Jamie spoke up. "Can I ask you something? Something personal?" He didn't take his eyes off the road.

Hailey turned to face him with a look of surprise. Something was definitely wrong. He seemed sad. She said "sure" as she tried to stay positive, but knew she came off as more confused than anything.

"How do you know you did the right thing...marrying your husband?"

The question sent a shock through her whole body. Why would he want to know that? She thought about telling him what everyone else would tell him. That you just know. When it's right, you'll just know it. But as she sat pondering what to say and why he was asking, she knew she had to tell him the truth or at least as close to her truth as she could without making things really uncomfortable between them. "I don't know that it was the right thing. I love him, always have, but I don't know that marrying him was the right thing to do. Sometimes I think it was the best decision I ever made. Other times I think it was the worst. I don't know." She paused for a moment and looked at him as he drove. "I'm not sure that one person can be everything we need for our whole lives. No matter how much we want them to be." Silence overwhelmed them once again. She knew she shouldn't, but she had to ask. "Is everything okay?"

"Yea. I just...I don't know. I guess I have just been thinking about it a lot lately. You know, wondering. Wondering if I did the right thing. Don't get me wrong, Amy's great. We're great, I just sometimes don't know if she was the one, you know?"

It was like a warm wave rolled over her and in that moment she felt both excited and horrified. The part of her that craved him was grinning from ear to ear hearing him say those words, but the part of her that loved Will so deeply and cared that Jamie was happy felt horrible guilt that he was clearly feeling so confused and that she found something exciting in it. She needed to know if she had anything to do with this and in a moment of pure desperation she said, "Can I ask you something personal now?"

"Shoot..."

She hesitated before speaking as if giving herself one last second to back out of what was definitely going to end up a messy situation one way or another. "Is there someone else?" When they had first met he seemed head over heels in love with Amy and over the last year, he just stopped talking about her. He didn't include her name in any of his stories anymore but he still seemed happy for the most part. She figured if your marriage is failing but you're still happy, there must be a reason and she desperately wanted to be that reason.

Jamie looked at her, slightly in shock, then back to the road. His hand left the steering wheel and adjusted his baseball cap. Then he put his hand over his mouth and rubbed his chin before putting it back on the wheel. "Yea. Shit."

He looked at Hailey with hurt in his eyes. Hurt for knowing this would cause pain for Amy, hurt for wanting someone he couldn't have. Hurt for being in the middle of something he didn't know how to handle.

"Jamie." She paused, knowing it probably wasn't the best idea to push this conversation but she couldn't help herself. "You don't have to hide from me. You can talk to me. There's obviously a lot going on in that head of yours." It was a moment that she knew could make or break her. She knew that what she felt for Jamie was more than any crush she had ever had, regardless of how often she tried to pretend it wasn't real. They were both married and the guilt of even thinking this way about him was enough to consume her, but no matter what she did or how many times she tried to stop, the thought of him was always there. She was terrified that he wasn't talking about her, and if he wasn't, then he didn't see her in that light at all; in fact, he saw someone else that way and she knew it would break her heart to find out. Against everything screaming inside her not to, she managed to choke out, "Tell me about her."

His eyes lit up and a smile appeared on his face. "She's amazing. She's just amazing. Beautiful as all hell but isn't afraid to get dirty. She has the biggest heart I've ever seen and she can be quiet which takes my breath away. I can't help but just want to watch her when she doesn't know I'm looking. She teases me and isn't afraid to put me in my place, but she does it in a way that just makes me want to be better for her. I feel like she just gets me. Like she's always been there, I just hadn't found her yet. Her horse is kinda out of the way but I make it work cause I can't stand the thought of not seeing her."

"She's a client?" Hailey said, with every nerve in her body on fire.

He nodded with a smile as he looked straight ahead out the windshield and just as fast as it had come on, the smile disappeared and he made a quick turn down a side road, pulling the truck over and stopping without saying a word. His hands didn't leave the wheel and she watched as the colour of his knuckles began to turn white. Even though she already couldn't take her eyes off of him, she turned her body towards him. Her heart was racing and her body felt riddled with panic.

"Jamie?"

"It's you," he said, turning to face her. "It's you. Of course it's you. Damit."

Shock set in and she couldn't speak. Even though that was the exact answer she had been hoping for, she couldn't react. How was she supposed to answer him, what was she supposed to say? She knew she felt the same way but how? How was it even possible that this was happening.

Jamie undid his seat belt and opened his door, getting out, leaving the door hanging open. He walked out in front of the truck and put his hands up on his head like he was about to scream. Hailey jumped out of the truck and walked over to him, putting her hand on his shoulder.

"Jamie...Jamie look at me," she said.

He put his hands down at his sides and turned toward her. The look of fear was all over his face and in that moment she had a choice to make. It was like time stopped and even though she had imagined this moment in one way or another since the day she first laid eyes on him, she didn't know what to do. In her daydreams she always chose to give in to him, but this was real and there would be real consequences. She closed her eyes and took a deep breath, deciding that the moment she opened them she would do what came naturally. Either turn and walk away or give in. Prepared as best as she could be to make that choice, she took one last deep breath and opened her eyes, looking straight into his. Her hand reached up toward his cheek and she felt his chiselled jaw in the palm of her hand. He placed his hand over hers and leaned his head a little into her touch.

"Jamie...I can't leave my husband." Tears welling up in her eyes.

His heart sank and his hand slipped from hers a slight bit, not quite letting go but holding on a little less.

Hailey took a deep breath in. "But I also can't just walk away from this. I fell for you the moment I laid eyes on you and for the life of me I can't shake it. God knows I've tried. You woke up a part of me that I didn't even know existed."

And there it was, her truth out in the open. Her soul bared to this man who came into her life by chance at a time she thought everything she knew was settled. She didn't expect this and never had the thought of cheating on Will ever crossed her mind until she met Jamie. In fact the thought still broke her heart but now it was as if she had two hearts. She was two different people living in the same body. A part of her very much craved the life she had built with Will and she loved him beyond words. But this past year and a half she had truly found herself and realized there was more to her than she had ever allowed to be known, even to herself. There was a side to her that just didn't fit in Wills world and although he did everything he could to help her live her dreams, he wasn't there to live them with her. He sometimes tagged along for the ride, but realistically, she was alone when it came to that part of her. Jamie took that loneliness away. He fit with that side of her like a glove and made the part of her that had felt so lonely for so long come alive. She didn't want to leave Will, but selfishly, she couldn't lose Jamie either.

"I don't want to walk away. I'll take any moment I can get with you," he said as he reached his hands up and placed them on either side of her face. And without hesitation and in a moment of pure need, they both leaned in hard as if it was the only way to save themselves. Their lips met and time stopped. Nothing else seemed to matter but each other and giving into this moment. As he pulled her in closer, it was as if the warm summer breeze decided to swirl around them in a dance.

When they finally allowed the kiss to end, they pulled back from each other just so slightly but not enough to let go of each other. The need to touch each other was too strong and had been waiting for too long. Her hands found their way to rest on his chest while he put one arm around her and the other he used to brush the hair from her forehead and tuck behind her ear.

"Why didn't you come on Sundays?" she said in the most heartbroken way. "I looked for you. You were never there."

He put his hand on the back of her hair and pulled her forehead to his lips, kissing her. "I wanted to. I really wanted to," he said, equally sounding heartbroken. "I didn't know what to think or what to do. The day you got hurt, it changed things. I mean everything before was innocent enough, at least that's what I thought, but that day...That day things changed. It wasn't innocent, and I realized none of it ever was. It just took that day to make me realize it. I had to leave when I did otherwise I would have kissed you right then and there and I didn't think you felt the same way. I didn't know."

She had pulled back to look in his eyes, hanging onto every word he spoke.

"I came back the next morning because I just couldn't stop myself. I had to see you again. I didn't have a job out your way."

"And then I told you I didn't need the help and you thought I was pushing you away?"

"Ya, more or less. I thought you might have guessed how I felt and were trying to let me know you didn't feel the same way."

"The moment those words came out of my mouth I felt like my heart broke. I didn't need the help, but I didn't mean to make it sound like I didn't want to see you. I didn't want you to leave but I also thought it was all in my head and it was getting to be too much for me, so I guess in a way I was pushing you away. I just didn't know it was hurting anyone but me. I said it all wrong and then I couldn't change what I said without making myself look like a fool if you weren't feeling what I was feeling and truthfully, I was scared to death of the thought that you were. I've spent the last month regretting ever speaking a word. I haven't been able to stop thinking about you and wanting to call you just to hear your voice."

He pulled her in close again and kissed her deeply before saying "Let's get you back home."

Once back in the truck he reached over and took her hand, squeezing it tight like he was afraid to let go. They didn't say much on the way back to her place, but

they never let go of each other's hands until they reached
the driveway to the farm.

"Will's at work?" he asked as he pulled into the
driveway.

"Yea, until about nine tonight." Suddenly she
realized that sounded like an invitation for things to go
about as far as they could. "Not that I'm saying anything
should...ah fuck, I should really just not speak," she said
with a slight laugh.

"No no, please, keep talking. I'd like to hear where
you were going with that," he teased.

She shot him some serious side-eye and welcomed
the fun playful way they were with each other. "I missed
this."

He pulled the truck up to the barn and turned it
off. "Am I allowed to kiss you here?" he asked, unsure of
when and where or even how they were going to go about
any of this.

Hailey nodded yes. "No one else is here to see. But
wait. Get out of the truck first."

Confused, but happily doing what she asked, Jamie
got out of the truck and met her at the door to the barn.
She walked in a few steps and turned to face him. "Here,"
she said with a smile.

He stopped in front of her and she reached up with
a slight amount of nervousness at how to go about
something so new, she put both arms around his neck
and just before she leaned in to kiss him, she whispered
in his ear "this is the spot we were standing the first time
we met."

Jamie stayed long enough to trim Charlie but
decided it was probably best if he didn't stick around too

long. He didn't want to push things with Hailey and wanted to make sure that when the time was right to be together completely, that it didn't come across as a fling or something he was pressuring her into. He had an idea but wanted to give her a night to sleep on it first. He wanted to make sure everything was perfect, besides, he wasn't keen on the idea of having that moment in the place she shared with someone else. They stood outside of his truck for almost an hour just talking and laughing. Unable to really keep their hands off each other until finally they had to break free.

"Okay, I really need to go. Seriously, if I don't go now, I won't go and that will be a bit of a problem," he said, grabbing her hands and holding them out away from him.

"I know. But...do I get to see you more than every six weeks? Or do I only get you when Charlie needs you?" She had started out with a smile, but it quickly faded as she realized that question was actually dead serious.

"We will figure something out. I promise." He really had no idea how they would make this work but he was willing to do whatever it took.

He kissed her one last time and went around to the drivers side of his truck and got in. As he pulled out down the laneway, dust flying up behind him, he stuck his hand out the window and waved goodbye.

Twelve

All My Life

Seven fifty am.

Jamie watched the clock as each minute passed. The closer it got to eight, the more nervous he became. His wife had left for work already and he thought he remembered Hailey once telling him that Will always left at eight.

Seven fifty one.

It hadn't even been twenty four hours since he had risked everything and told Hailey how he felt about her and he knew they had no solid idea of how this was going

to work. They had a lot to talk about and all that aside,
he just needed to see her.

Seven fifty-three.

Hailey was busying herself around the kitchen,
unable to get yesterday's events out of her mind. She was
trying to be present with Will and keep him from guessing
anything was any different but she kept finding herself
distracted. Thankfully he was running late this morning
so he didn't have a lot of time for talking.

Seven fifty-eight.

She watched the clock, waiting for eight o'clock but
in reality, didn't know what she was going to do when Will
walked out the door for work. She wanted to talk to
Jamie. She wanted to see him and kiss him again but she
was terrified. What if he had changed his mind? What if
seeing his wife after he left her place last night had
changed things for him? Made him feel like he made a
mistake? She was a nervous wreck.

Eight o'clock.

Jamie picked up his phone, paced through his
kitchen and then put it back down on the counter.
Nervous to call her in case Will was still home, he decided
to give it another twenty minutes. He headed out to the
barn and took care of Joe to distract himself. It felt like it
took forever to get everything done that he needed to do
but when he looked at his phone, thinking it had been too
long already, he saw only eleven minutes had passed.

Eight thirteen.

Will kissed Hailey on the cheek like he did every morning before heading out the door. She watched as he got in his car and pulled away from the house and out of sight.

Eight fifteen.
She walked back into the kitchen and put her hands on the counter on either side of her phone. 'Just call him' she thought. She stood up straight and ran her hands through her hair out of frustration.

"Agh" she sighed and she stepped outside on the porch. Barn chores were needing to get done and she wasn't doing herself any favours sitting in the house staring at her phone. She headed down the porch steps towards the barn.

Eight nineteen.
He couldn't wait anymore. If Will was still there she would just have to figure out what to tell him. He needed to hear her voice.

Eight nineteen.
She heard her phone ring from the kitchen and she turned and ran back into the house. Leaving the porch door swinging as she reached the counter, she saw his name on her call display. As she reached for it she felt all her nervousness melt away.

The phone rang three times before finally, he heard her say "hi."

"Hi," he said, unable to stop smiling at the sound of her voice. "Is this a bad time?"

"No, it's good. I'm alone. You?"

"Yea, me too. Listen I have an idea if you're up for it."

"I'm up for anything if it means I get to see you," she said before she could even think.

"You don't have your truck right?"

"No, it's still at the garage. They should call later today."

"Ok, can I pick you up? There's somewhere I want to take you for a few hours. Think you can get away?"

"Will's gone until about five o'clock. As long as I'm back before that, yes!"

"I'll be there soon," he said before hanging up.

Shoving her phone in her pocket, she ran out to do her morning chores. Fed Charlie and turned her out, leaving her stall to clean later on.

It wasn't more than twenty minutes later that she heard his truck coming up the laneway. She took a deep breath as he pulled up in front of her. He jumped out and came around the passenger side of his truck, grabbing her up in his arms and kissing her like he hadn't thought of a single other thing since he left her standing in that very spot the night before.

When they finally broke free from each other's desperate embrace, she bit her bottom lip. As if that somehow allowed the moment to last just that much longer.

Jamie took a step toward the truck and opened the passenger side door for her. Without either of them saying a word, Hailey walked over and got in the truck. The silence held more intent than any words could actually mean and she knew that wherever he was taking her was where he was going to make her his.

He jumped in and put the truck in drive, pulling around to head back out the laneway.

"You should probably pay attention to the way we go," he said. "I'd rather the address not be written down in case it gets seen by anyone else."

"I take it you're hoping this won't be the only time we go here?"

He turned and looked at her with a smile. "Better not be."

They drove out past where her truck had broken down the day before and kept on going. About fifteen minutes later he pulled onto a private dirt drive that looked like it hadn't seen a vehicle on it in years. They turned a corner and she saw an old log cabin come into view. Like the road there, it looked like it hadn't been touched in years.

"This is the cabin you told me about yesterday?" she asked.

"No one comes here," he said, parking the truck in front of the porch. They opened their doors and stepped out.

Hailey could see the lake peeking through the trees just behind the cabin. "It's beautiful."

"It was my Grandad's," he said as he looked around. "Haven't really been here since he left it to me."

She realized that this place meant the world to him but what she couldn't quite figure out was why, if it meant so much, he didn't come here..

"Come on," he said, reaching for her hand. He led her up the steps toward the front door. Unlocking it, he swung it open and took a step inside. Hailey followed him in and pulled the door closed behind her. It was a small place and didn't look to have much in the way of anything modern.

"This place..." he began. "This is the only place I know no one will look for us."

Hailey looked around the one-room cabin, taking a few steps past Jamie, she moved toward the old stone fireplace that was obviously the centrepiece of the whole cabin. A small loveseat type couch covered with an old bed sheet faced it on her right side, a wooden table and two chairs sat just behind the couch to her left. Then her eyes looked toward the back wall of the cabin, close enough to the fireplace to feel the warmth, but not so close as to feel like it was in the way, was a double bed with an old throw blanket draped over top. She knew he saw her looking at it and she knew why he had brought her here. Taking one last glance at the bed, she tried to make a mental note of the moment. She knew it was one she wouldn't ever want to forget. That bed was the place she was going to lose herself in him.

She turned to face him and saw the look of desperation in his eyes. She needed him in that moment more than she had ever needed anything or anyone else. He was the last piece of her puzzle and the thought of either of them deciding to walk away from this moment was more than she could bear. She began to breathe deeply and with each rush of air in her lungs, her body ached for him. As if a magnet to her, he ignored all the reason's he shouldn't and he came at her, grabbing ahold of the sides of her face with his strong hands and kissing her like he needed to drown in her. They stumbled backwards into the wall beside the bed. Their bodies as close to each other as they could get. He ran his hands down her shoulders, sliding down her arms to her fingertips. Letting their fingers intertwine before he put his hands on either side of her waist, pulling her hips toward his. She reached her arms up and wrapped them around his neck, letting her fingers find their way to run through his hair. He stopped kissing her and moved back, just enough that he could see her. He reached for the bottom of her shirt and pulled it up over her head. She couldn't help but smile and bit the side of her bottom lip again. He quickly pulled off his tee-shirt before reaching down, placing his hands on the backs of her thighs and lifting her up, wrapping her legs around his waist. He kissed her deeply while he carried her the three steps to the bed and laid her down on her back, climbing up on top of her.

She hadn't really known what to expect and now that she was in the moment, she realized it was far more intense than she could have ever possibly imagined. Every touch sent shivers down her spine, every breath made her weak. She held onto him like he was the only thing that could keep her alive as the rest of their clothes made their way to the floor and their bodies collided like they somehow always knew they were meant to be together. The way his skin felt against hers was like coming home, as if this moment was long ago lost and finally found again.

In the end, he kissed her softly and brushed her hair from her face. He rolled off to the side of her, never looking away from her eyes. How she felt like she was already madly in love with this man, she didn't know, but she couldn't look away. Nothing so wrong had ever felt so right. She reached up and touched the side of his face, running her fingers along the stubble on his jaw line as if to memorize every inch of him. She had so much she wanted to say to him but all she could do was reach up and gently graze his lips with hers.

Knowing the moment couldn't last forever he finally spoke.

"I have no idea how I'm supposed to drop you back off after this." He sat up, swinging his legs off the side of the bed and pulling the sheet over his lap.

Hailey sat up behind him, wrapped her arms around his chest laying her cheek against his back. "I know," she said, her heart feeling like it was about to break. Tears welling up in her eyes, she fought them back, sat up and moved around him, pulling the beds throw blanket off and wrapping it around herself. She crouched down on the floor in front of him. "Look at me," she said, placing her hands back on the sides of his face to make sure he couldn't do anything but hear her out. "Whatever this is with us, it's ours. No one can take this away from us. From the moment I met you, I knew you, like you were a god damn part of me from the very beginning. I don't know how to do this and I know a lot of it is going to feel like torture. But this..." she paused "...this is worth every bit of it. You're going to drop me back off and you're going to drive away and at first it's going to feel like shit. Then you're going to smile and replay every detail and every moment we just shared like it's a movie in your head." She began to smile. "And then you're going to realize that you just blew off an entire days work to make love to me in your cabin and now you have to spend the rest of the week trying to catch up." She laughed, realizing that it was probably a really bad move, but like she had just told him, it was all worth it.

He finally cracked a smile and reached down to lift her up on his lap. Sitting on his knee, with her legs between his and her arms around his neck, he rested his hand on her lap and looked into her eyes. "You're amazing," he said before he kissed her lips gently.

They stood up and began to get dressed. She hadn't felt nervous the entire time they were making love, but for some reason, she felt incredibly vulnerable standing in front of him putting her clothes back on.

"Guess we should probably make the bed," she said as she pulled her boots on. She reached for the sheets and started to straighten them but soon realized he wasn't coming over to help her. She glanced back over her shoulder to see him standing near the table. He smiled when she made eye contact with him.

"Jamie Sutton, are you staring at my ass!?"

"It's a good ass." He said teasing her before finally walking over to help her make the bed the rest of the way.

Once the place was back to looking the way it was when they got there, they headed for the door. He opened it and stepped to the side, placing his hand on her lower back to guide her to the porch. She stepped out and turned towards him, grabbing a hold of the back of his shirt as he pulled the door closed and locked it up.

He reached back and grabbed her hand, sliding hers inside his and walked her to the truck. He opened the door for her the same way he did the day before when her truck broke down, before either of them had allowed themselves to be truthful about how they felt. He closed it once she was in and came around to the driver side. Jumping in and starting the truck, he pulled away from the cabin. She watched it slowly disappear in the dust through the side mirror hoping with everything she had in her that it wouldn't be the last time she was here.

The drive to her place didn't take nearly as long as she needed it to and before she knew it they were pulling up in front of her house. Thankfully, to a still empty driveway. Although she hadn't ever known Will to come home early, after all, each of his classes were on a set schedule, she knew, especially after what had happened today, that you just can't predict life. They were going to have to be more careful and somehow plan things out so they didn't get caught.

She undid her seatbelt and turned her body toward him. Looking into his eyes she took a long deep breath before saying "well this isn't easy!"

Thirteen

Unprofessional

Over the course of the next six weeks, Hailey and Jamie had found a way to sneak off to the cabin at least once a week. When they couldn't find enough time throughout the rest of the week to make their way there, they would meet up in whatever area Jamie was working that day, pull off on a side road somewhere and make out like teenagers until his next appointment.

Hailey was feeling like life was being breathed back into her. It was a drug that she just couldn't get enough of.

She tried to make things at home seem like nothing had changed, although it was harder to manage than she anticipated. Trying to find time to write was also proving to be hard and she had lied to Will a few times about how she had spent her day. He never read her writing in the past and wouldn't start now, so she used it as her constant alibi.

"How was your day?" Will would ask when he got home from work.

"Oh, not too exciting. I spent most of the day writing," she would say.

She even became nervous to write Jamie's name on the calendar in the kitchen, even though she had always written his name on the dates Charlie was due for a visit with him. So when she realized it had almost been six weeks since his name appeared on the calendar, she grabbed her phone with an actual reason to text Jamie.

"Charlie would love to see you near the end of the week. When can you fit her in?" she wrote.

Almost instantly, which was a bit of a surprise, he wrote back. *"Friday at noon? I have the whole afternoon open so I can spend a little extra time with her."*

Hailey smiled, knowing that neither was talking about Charlie.

"Perfect. She'll be ready and waiting for you."

She never wanted their conversations to end, but they had both agreed to keep things short and sweet and to delete any of their conversations that didn't have to do with Charlie's appointments as soon as they were done talking. And in case their spouses were with them when the messages came in, they never said anything right away they couldn't explain.

Hailey grabbed a pen and jotted his name down on the calendar for Friday. Oddly, she feared that she had somehow written his name differently and that Will would notice.

Friday rolled around and Hailey's mood was on a high. She had been up early and had made Will breakfast. Instead of sitting to eat with him, she grabbed a piece of bacon off his plate as she set it down in front of him and headed back to the counter to make him a lunch for work.

"What's up with you these days?" he asked.

"What do you mean?"

"You have been running around here like a kid in a candy store lately. You finish your book or something?"

"No, not yet. I don't know. Just happy I guess." she said smiling at him.

"Well whatever it is, I hope it keeps up. It's nice seeing you like this every day."

Suddenly Hailey realized that he was right. She was happy, all the time. She hadn't actually felt this happy in a while, even though things were seemingly going well with her and Will, the farm, his job and her books. There was just always something missing and she could never put her finger on it. And then Jamie walked into her life. It was him and everything he brought out in her that was making this change. He woke her up and made her feel excitement for each day, whether she was seeing him or not. She was just happy. However, the irony wasn't lost on her that Will was asking her to keep Jamie around without realizing what his request actually meant.

Will headed to work and Hailey headed to the barn. She did her chores and tacked up Charlie for a ride in the warm sun. She headed down the trail she had taken with Jamie the day she fell, this time paying close attention not to fall or have Charlie spook. Passing the spot he had jumped from Joe and ran to her side, picking her up in his arms and holding her. The moments played out like a movie in her mind. The way his hands felt, grazing against her bare skin and how she couldn't help but react in the moment. Knowing that she got to see him later felt like a gift she didn't deserve, but she wasn't going to pass it up for anything.

As she headed back to the barn, she found herself becoming lost in her guilt. Will's comment that morning had struck a nerve she didn't see coming. How could she be so happy? She was living life by the 'what they don't know won't kill them' rule. But she knew, and she knew what it would do to Will if he found out. She was having her cake and eating it too and suddenly her guilt overwhelmed her. It had gone too far...hell it had started out too far in the first place! She didn't know if she believed in fate or destiny or whatever you want to call it, she just knew that where Jamie was concerned, she felt like she never had a choice. He came out of nowhere and made her whole. Yet somehow, she still felt just as much love for Will as she always had. It was just a different love, from a different part of her.

She got back to the barn just before eleven and left Charlie in a stall. Jamie would be there in about an hour so she ran to the house for a quick shower and to tidy up around the house. He had never come in further than the kitchen door and she didn't really have any intention of asking him to since she figured it would make him uncomfortable, but she welcomed the distraction of cleaning to pass the time and keep her mind from dwelling on everything she had been thinking about during her ride.

At noon on the dot, she heard Jamie's truck driving up the laneway. She tossed the blankets on the couch that she was in the middle of folding and ran for the door. In the off chance that anyone pulled in behind him, she reserved her hello hug and kiss for inside the barn. He got out of the truck and greeted her with a smile. She tucked her hair coyly behind her ear and smiled back.

"She's in the barn already," Hailey said, motioning with a nod for him to follow her in.

Once inside, Jamie grabbed the back of Hailey's jeans and pulled her backward into him. He wrapped his arms around her as he leaned back on one of the stall doors. The hair she had tucked behind her ear moments before allowed him clear access to kiss the side of her neck.

"Jamie Sutton, this is so unprofessional of you." She joked.

Letting each kiss linger just a little bit longer along the side of her neck, hoping to make a point, he said, "I can stop if you want me to."

Arching her neck to the left, giving him not only more room, but the reaction he had clearly been going for, she let out a quiet moan. "No, that's quite okay," she whispered.

With his hands already on her waist, he started grazing his fingertips along her stomach just at the top of her jeans, letting them slip under the bottom of her shirt. She felt her whole world start to slip away and all she could focus on was how his hands felt on her and how desperately he was making her want more. Her body became covered in goosebumps as he inched his way just under the top of her jeans, and just as she was about to forget all the reasons this was probably a bad idea and how they could far too easily be caught out in the open like this, he pulled his hands away, stopped kissing her neck and stood up straight, stepping out around her and headed in the direction of Charlie's stall.

"So Charlie...ready for your trim?" he asked, trying not to laugh.

Hailey's mouth fell open and she looked at him with surprise. Turning to see the look on her face, he smiled at her obvious flustered reaction.

"You are so going to pay for that," she said.

"I'm really hoping so Darlin'."

She loved it when he called her Darlin'.

Jamie finished up Charlie's trim and after Hailey gave her a carrot, he turned her out in the field. Hailey couldn't help but realize that Will never did anything like that. He was married to her and she had said a million times over that Charlie was theirs. He just never took the opportunity to really do anything with her. Even something as small as putting her out for the day. Jamie had done this a few times now and she couldn't help but feel like she shared more of Charlie with him than she did her own husband.

He came back into the barn and headed for the small bathroom to wash up.

"I brought you something," He said as he turned off the light and closed the door.

"You didn't have to bring me anything."

"I know, but I figured it was about time we had a proper date. All we do when we find time together is…well…" He looked at her with eyes that said 'you know exactly what we do when we're together and it sure as hell isn't date'.

"Well if you insist!" she said with an excited smile.

He headed out to his truck and came back in with a large black bag.

"Wait here. I'll call you when I'm ready," he said as he began to climb the ladder that led to the hayloft.

Completely unsure of what he was up to, she waited patiently as he had asked. It had been a long time since she had been on a proper date and the thought of spending time with him, regardless of what they were doing made her happy.

He had been up there about five minutes before he hollered down for her to come up. As she came to the top of the ladder and peaked up inside the loft she was taken back by what she saw.

The loft had been transformed into a picnic lunch, complete with candles and flowers.

"Oh Jamie," she said, walking toward him. "This is amazing."

He took her hand and led her to the middle of the blanket he had laid out and had her sit down. He sat next to her and started unwrapping packages of food and pulled out two cold beers from a cooler.

"You've thought of everything," she said. "Right down to the battery operated candles!"

"Well, I didn't want to burn your barn down."

"Thanks," she said with a little laugh. "Appreciate it."

After eating, they moved the rest of the food out of the way and laid down together with Hailey's head resting on Jamie's shoulder. They spent the rest of the afternoon up in the loft, just talking and telling each other all the small details about their lives that they never really thought to tell anyone. With hesitation in her voice, Hailey decided to finally ask him the one question that had been on her mind since the beginning. "Can I ask you something? Something that might be personal."

"Sure."

"Why didn't you ever go to your cabin before you met me? You obviously care about it a lot, but you made it sound like you've avoided it."

"I guess because I did avoid it." His tone sounded sad. It was obviously a painful thing for him to talk about because he didn't offer up a real answer right away.

"It's okay if you don't want to talk about it." She didn't want to push him. They had been through and talked about some pretty deep stuff together and the fact that the cabin hadn't come up told her it was something he felt strongly about.

"It was my Grandads. I spent most of my summers there with him when I was a kid. It was kind of like a second home to me."

Hailey sat up next to him so she could see him face to face.

"I could always tell when something wasn't right with him, he would go there and put a fire on in the fireplace and just sit, staring at the flames. Didn't matter much what the weather was outside. Somehow it seemed to let him think things through better. He burned a lot of fires in that old stone fireplace after my Gram passed; then when I was seventeen, he had a heart attack sitting at the kitchen table in the cabin." He paused for a long while and she didn't dare break the silence because she knew he wasn't finished.

"I found out soon after that he had left the cabin to me. I was only a kid and I didn't know what to do with it. I didn't want to go there because it reminded me too much of him but I couldn't sell it either. So I closed it up. I never even told Amy it existed and no one in my family even brings it up anymore. I go there once every year just to check on it and do any work that needs to be done, but until you, I hadn't spent any time there."

He reached out and picked up her hand that had been laying on his chest. Rubbing his thumb into her palm as he held it.

"Why did you bring me there?" she asked, hoping he hadn't felt forced to.

"It just felt right. I don't know. I didn't question it, it was the first place that came to mind when I thought of where I wanted to be with you."

Hailey smiled and leaned in to kiss him. As she laid back down next to him, she said "I'm really glad you wanted me there. I like being a part of your world."

Before they knew it, it was almost five o'clock and Will would be home soon. They packed up the candles, blanket and leftover food and put it all back in the bag he brought it in, before heading back down the ladder into the barn. She headed down first, just to be on the safe side and when she saw that she didn't have any surprise visitors, she called for him to come down. He put the bag back in his truck and came back in the barn to give her a goodbye kiss.

"I guess I'll have to get you back for earlier another time," she said.

"Oh, I'm looking forward to it," he said with a smile before taking a few steps to the door. Suddenly, he turned around and came back, taking both her hands in his.

"I know this is maybe really fast, and I don't want to scare you off, but Hailey..." he paused, looking at her like he just couldn't believe it, a smile crept across his face and he continued, "...I am so insanely in love with you."

She stood silently staring into his eyes, taking in how perfect that moment was.

"You don't have to say it back," he said. "I just need you to know how I feel."

"Jamie, I have loved you since the day I first met you. I don't know how, it was just there; as if it had always been. As if you had always been there and how I feel about you has only gotten stronger over time and now I don't know how I ever lived without you."

He leaned in and kissed her, lifting her off her feet one last time before he turned and headed out the door, getting in his truck and driving off.

She stood outside the barn door and watched him head out the laneway. His hand reaching out the window to wave goodbye as he got close to out of sight, the way he always did.

Hailey hadn't even made it across the driveway before she saw Will coming toward the house. She panicked like a deer in headlights because she knew that Jamie wouldn't have had time to make it out before Will was there. Calming herself, she ran through everything in her head. Jamie was supposed to be there for Charlie that day. It had been on the calendar for a few days. There wasn't a time written down so it wasn't like he would ask why it took so long. There hadn't been enough time for them to have stopped and spoken, so there was no need to worry. Although everything in her body screamed otherwise.

"Hey," Will said as he got out of his car. "Jamie actually showed up when he was supposed to."

"What?" Hailey asked, sounding shocked as she slowly walked up the steps to the porch.

"Jamie. Well, I assume that's who that was pulling out of the laneway? He showed up the day he was supposed to. That never happens."

"Oh, right. Ya, he made it on time today." She turned to face the house and took a deep breath trying to get a hold of herself. She had never had to see Will within seconds of Jamie before and it was throwing her for a bit of a loop.

They walked into the house and Will set his bag down on the island in the kitchen.

"Any plans for dinner tonight?" he asked.

"I'm not actually that hungry. I think I want to grab a shower though if you don't mind. I can make you something when I'm out if you want to wait?"

"I'll whip something up. You go shower."

Hailey smiled at him and walked down the hall to their room. She grabbed a change of clothes, yoga pants and a long sleeved tee shirt and headed to the bathroom. She didn't usually lock the door but did this time. She needed a moment to breath where she couldn't be caught having what felt like a full blown panic attack.

Hailey turned the water on but didn't get in the shower right away. She turned the volume down on her phone so Will wouldn't hear it if Jamie wrote back.

"Will pulled in right after you left! Did you run into him? Did he say anything to you?"

She knew he would still be driving and hoped he would get the message before he went in his house. A few seconds later he had written her back.

"Ya that was a little too close for comfort. I was just pulling out onto the road when he was pulling in so I just kept going. Everything okay?"

"Ya, he doesn't suspect anything. I felt like I was about to suffocate though so I told him I needed to grab a shower. I've locked myself in the bathroom. By the way, thank you again for today. It was amazing. I clearly don't deserve it."

"Everything will be okay. Don't worry. Just grab u shower and take a minute for yourself. I'm just going to go home and pretend I'm not jealous as all hell that I'm not the one you're spending your evening with."

"These days, it's not you that needs to be jealous." She hadn't even thought before writing it but it really was true. Will may have noticed that she had been happier and seemed to have more energy, but it had no effect on their sex life. In fact, it was kind of the opposite. They were starting to grow apart in that way. It wasn't the first time they had lost that level of intimacy, so she knew it wasn't something Will would look for a reason for.

"Good to know." he wrote back

"I'm sorry, that was more than you wanted to know. Okay, I'm going to grab a shower. Let me know when you can get away next. I can't wait to see you."

"Night Darlin."

She quickly deleted all of their messages before she stepped into the shower. She washed her hair and turned the water off. She had wasted a lot of time texting Jamie

and she knew it would be a little too long if she actually
just stood under the water any longer like she wanted to.
She dressed and towel dried her hair, quietly unlocked the
door in the hope that Will wouldn't notice that she had
locked it in the first place, and walked into the kitchen
where he was just about finished cooking.

"Smells good," she said.

Will looked over at her. "Feel better?"

"Much!"

"Hungry?"

"Ya, a little I guess."

"I figured you would be."

"You know me pretty well," she said smiling at him.

They grabbed their plates and sat down at the table
together. They didn't really talk about anything
important, just made random small talk. The 'how was
your day?' kind. Finally, Will asked how long it was until
Amanda's wedding.

"SHIT," Hailey yelled. "Oh my god, I've been so
busy that I have been the worst friend." She jumped up
from her chair and ran to the calendar. "Two weeks from
tomorrow. It's two friggin weeks from tomorrow and I
have been so out to lunch. Damn it."

"I'm sure she understands. If she needed
something, she would let you know. It is Amanda we're
talking about after all."

Hailey felt guilty that she had been so wrapped up
in her own world that she had completely lost track of
how little time there was left until the wedding. Amanda
hadn't wanted a bridal party, but if there was the role of
Maid Of Honour, Hailey would have been it.

Fourteen

Wedding Bells

The night of Amanda's wedding was as perfect as you could wish for on a late August summer night. Strings of vintage light bulbs hanging in the trees lit the night with a romantic glow. Seats made of hay bales and blankets were scattered around the outsides of the wooden dance floor overlooking the lake. The bar was open; of course, and it seemed everyone from town had been invited.

Hailey, dressed in a light blue floral dress that showed off every curve of her body, without being over the top, and brown cowboy boots, felt oddly out of place and struggled to truly enjoy the evening. She knew a few people and causally mingled but for the most part, she stayed close to Will; flashbacks of their own wedding popping through her mind like lightning bolts. Being at a wedding had made her question everything. Her guilt was like the weight of the world and she desperately wished she could come clean to Will, but she knew the consequences if she did. It would end them and that wasn't a thought she could bear. Feeling overwhelmed by all of the emotions the night had brought on, she turned toward the band to attempt a moment of peace and just like that, there he was. Jamie. It was either karma or fate, she wasn't quite sure, but the feeling in the pit of her stomach told her she didn't care which it was. She had never expected to see him there, and for a moment, she forgot that Will was standing right next to her. Then the gut-wrenching realization sunk in that Jamie was there with his wife. She watched from the other side of the dance floor as a beautiful, thin brunette walked up to Jamie's side and tucked in close, while his hand, without thought, reached up and rested on the small of her back. Hailey's heart sank. Feeling heat rising up her spine, confusion set in. She felt dizzy and unprepared for this moment. It's not like she didn't know he was married, but she had never imagined being in a situation where she had to watch him be someone else's. Her heart was beating so hard she thought for sure Will would notice. Looking away, she hoped Jamie hadn't seen her yet, begging he wouldn't approach her if and when he did. In her panic, she let go of Will's hand and turned toward the lake, hoping to keep her back to Jamie and her inevitably alarmed look away from Will's line of sight until she could get hold of herself. Realizing Will was too caught up in his conversation to notice, she took the time to catch her breath and come up with a game plan. Will knew Jamie existed, although she didn't think he would recognize him. Maybe Will would never find out Jamie was there, but if he did, if someone said his name in passing, and Will overheard...He knew she had a working relationship with Jamie and it would be weird if she acted like he was a stranger or even just an acquaintance. She would have to say hello, all while standing next to Will and more than likely, heartbreakingly, meet Jamie's wife. They had always agreed they would never cross those lines, but aside from faking sick and telling Will they needed to leave, she didn't see any other way.

She took a deep breath and turned back toward Will. With her heart still racing, she glanced back toward Jamie. This time, he saw her, and with their eyes locked on each other, it was as if they could speak without words. Both terrified their relationship would come to light, both hurt by the sight of the other with their spouse, both equally longing for each other in the most desperate of ways.

"Hailey!" Will said sharply.

Panic set in. Her body reacted with a startle as her gaze turned quickly back to Will. Had he noticed who she was looking at? Had he questioned why she was acting so strange? Did he know?

"Yes?" She managed to get out with a quirky yet unconvincing smile.

"Daydreaming? I just asked you three times if you wanted a drink."

"Uh, no. I'm fine. Actually; on second thought, a drink would be great!" She needed to calm her nerves.

Will laughed to himself as he walked past her toward the bar and as she kept her attention on him walking away, she knew she had to get it together or this night would turn disastrous.

She smelled him before she heard him. That amazing cologne that reminded her of every muscle in his body and the way his hands would run down her sides to her hips, pulling her in close. She closed her eyes and breathed deeply; no need to turn around, he was there.

"You okay?" Jamie asked quietly from behind her. He stood off to the side a bit and faced slightly towards the dance floor, just to make sure it didn't look like he was there to talk to her.

"No," she said, looking around at all the guests. Hoping no one was actually looking at her or they would think she was talking to herself. "Will is at the bar and I don't know how to do this. Why are you here? I saw Amanda's guest list. You weren't on it."

"Amy knows Amanda's husband, through work I guess. She got the invite. She's never gone by my last name."

Hailey took some kind of comfort in that knowledge. She was pretty traditional and thought that when a woman didn't take her husband's last name, it sort of felt like she was keeping her distance so to speak.

"She hadn't said anything to me about it until a few days ago and for some reason I got the date mixed up and thought she was talking about a wedding that was a few weeks away." He paused and took a moment to steal a glance at Hailey before looking away again toward the lake. "Listen, it's going to be fine, but Will knows we aren't strangers so we have to eventually say hi or it will be awkward."

"I know. I just..." she cleared her throat, feeling tears building behind her eyes. "Please don't make me meet her." Hailey's voice trembled as the words came tumbling out.

He stepped around to face her and smiled like he just noticed she was there. "Deep breath and keep smiling okay? We'll get through this."

He reached up and put his strong warm hand on her shoulder. "By the way, you look unbelievable tonight." The feeling of him touching her skin was almost more than she could bear.

"See ya around," he said with a smile letting his hand slowly slide from her shoulder as he walked off toward the bar, passing Will on his way there. The sight of the two of them literally in the same place at the same time was enough to take the wind right out of her. How was he so calm about all of this!? How had he managed to get it together in mere moments. She was sure when they first saw each other that he looked as broken as she did.

"Who was that?" Will asked as he handed Hailey a beer.

"Huh? Oh, that was Jamie. Small world." She tried to force a smile that said she was surprised to have bumped into him, but she couldn't quite shake the feeling that she just looked like a deer forever in headlights.

"So that's the mysterious Jamie. In the flesh!" Will said as he turned to glance one more time at Jamie.

"Mysterious?"

"Yea. The guys at my house every five or six weeks yet I've never actually met him. I was beginning to wonder if you hadn't made him up."

Hailey chuckled a little nervous laugh and took a big swig of her beer. She knew Will didn't suspect anything but his insecure nature was bound to show through, especially now that he had laid eyes on Jamie. It wasn't as if he couldn't see for himself that the guy was pretty much textbook 'western dream guy' material and he knew that world was very much a part of who Hailey was.

Jamie had finished at the bar and was heading back their way. Hailey's eyes widened with fear, confused why he wasn't even trying to avoid them; he could have walked another way. Was this about to be some sort of alpha male pissing contest, where she was the prize on the table? She couldn't fathom Jamie would be that bold, especially given how scared he knew she was about this entire situation. He wouldn't do that to her, she knew he wouldn't, so why? Maybe it was his own self-torture; a way to punish himself for falling in love with another woman, to test himself perhaps, to see if this was really something he could continue to do. As luck would have it, the band began playing a slow song and although Hailey didn't recognize it, she quickly grabbed Wills hand and headed for the dance floor, avoiding Jamie; chugging back the last of her beer before setting the bottle down on a table as they went. They stepped up onto the wooden platform and Will pulled her in close. He was never the type of guy to dance with her in an old traditional way. He never took her hand in his, it was always the high school type of dance where he had both hands on her waist and her arms around his neck. She didn't mind, at least he would dance with her which is more than can be said for a lot of the husbands there that night.

With her cheek pressed against Wills, she closed her eyes and tried to shut off her fear and nerves and enjoy the moment, not so much for her sake, but for Will's. It wasn't too often they got to spend this kind of time together but she found it spoke volumes that Jamie was there. She opened her eyes and as Will turned her around on the dance floor, holding her close, she once again locked eyes with Jamie. He was standing behind his wife while she chatted away with a friend, and he was watching Hailey's every move. She saw the pain in his eyes and couldn't help but feel horrible for dancing with her own husband. She desperately wanted to whisper 'I'm sorry', even just to mouth it in his direction, but couldn't risk it being noticed by the wrong person who might have an eagle eye view of the person on the receiving end of it.

"It's been a while since we danced," Will said.

Hailey leaned back so she could see him face to face.

"It has. Probably a few years. I wasn't sure you still knew how." She smiled, trying to break the tension she felt inside but only succeeded in adding more. She was torn, she couldn't avoid her husband to keep Jamie from feeling pain, but at the same time, she was breaking to be causing him that pain. It was torture and she just wanted to run.

By the time the song came to its end, everything in her was screaming to leave but she couldn't do that to Amanda. She had already failed when it came to helping her with planning the wedding, leaving it early wasn't an option. She had gotten herself into this mess and so she would need to figure out how to deal with it.

"I'll be right back. Washroom break," she said to Will as they walked off the dance floor. She hoped that once Jamie saw her excuse herself toward the washroom that he would follow with the same excuse, giving them a chance to talk, but as luck would have it, when she walked past where he was standing, out of the corner of her eye she saw his wife grab ahold of his arm to introduce him to someone she was talking to.

      The wedding was held at the town's main park so thankfully they had nice accommodations as far as washrooms went. With any other outdoor wedding she had been to, it was always porta potties that no girl in a dress could actually manage to use properly. It was a far enough distance away that she knew she was buying herself a little time to figure out what to do, but it wouldn't be enough time for Jamie to finish with his new conversation, make it over to her and have enough time for the two of them to talk. Looking in the mirror she realized she had a choice to make. Be a less than perfect friend or risk her marriage. She knew it wasn't really a choice; the cake cutting would be soon and since she had been there for the ceremony, dinner and most of the reception at that point, she decided to bite the bullet and sneak out once the bride and groom had successfully smushed cake in each other's faces, hoping Amanda would be too wrapped up in her night to notice Hailey's semi-early exit. Regardless, she would have to deal with the consequences of burning bridges in friendships after she managed to stop a fire from starting where her love life was concerned.

      Leaving the washroom she realized that she had a good view of the wedding without having to really be a part of it. She walked slowly toward the crowd, some seated, some dancing and some standing in small circles chatting away. She saw Will talking to Collin near the bar, seeming to have a great time. Glancing to the other side of the party, she laid eyes on Jamie, still standing with his wife as she talked away to other guests she knew.

It dawned on Hailey that aside from her and Amanda, he didn't know a soul here; and he barely knew Amanda, nor did she even seem to know he was there. She had never pictured Jamie as the quiet guy in social settings, but she soon realized that this wasn't his setting. This was Amy's. He was out of place the same way Hailey felt out of place at Will's staff Christmas party last winter.

She watched him for a little longer, seeing him scan the crowd, wondering if he was looking for her. His gaze landed on Will and it seemed he couldn't look away. As Hailey got closer to Will, Jamie saw her; he watched her walk to Will and smile as he welcomed her back. She hugged Collin and congratulated him once again and then positioned herself so she could see Jamie without having to turn around completely. He was still watching her, although she didn't need to see it to know. She could feel his eyes on her, burning into her, a mix of anger, desire and fear.

The DJ announced the cake cutting and everyone moved toward the cake stand. The Groom was just about the last person to make it there since he had been standing so far back with Will and Hailey. Laughter and applause erupted as he made his way to the front and Collin and Amanda cut two slices of cake, intertwining their arms to feed each other a piece. Luckily, Collin knew better than to actually rub cake in Amanda's face and simply faked the gesture to please the crowd, but then romantically promised her he would be kind and gently held it out for her to take a bite.

Hailey leaned into Will to whisper in his ear. "We should probably get going now. It's getting late." She couldn't stand the thought of hurting Jamie and after seeing the look on his face while she danced with Will, she knew this was truly just as hard on him as it was her, regardless of how well he seemed like he had it together when they spoke. She also didn't want to stick around for the moment his wife decided she wanted to dance with him. It wasn't something Hailey could handle; but before she could get Will to leave, the DJ started to play another song. It was their song, the one they had their first dance to at their wedding. Swallowing hard she hoped Will hadn't noticed.

"Hey, isn't this our song?" he asked.

Hailey smiled and Will grabbed her hand, leading her to the dance floor. As luck would have it, Will walked her right to a spot on the dance floor that gave her a clear view of Jamie. Only a few feet away from him, she could almost see his heart pounding. He looked hurt and angry and all she wanted to do was stop his pain. She closed her eyes so she couldn't see him anymore. If she kept looking she was going to do something she would regret and that wouldn't do anyone any favours. The song seemed to last for a ridiculous amount of time and each sway she took in Will's arms made her heart ache and her stomach turn.

The song ended and Will slid his hands from Hailey's waist and caught her hand by the pinkie. She opened her eyes but refused to look anywhere but down toward the floor. She forced a stressed smile and slid her hand into Will's. They walked off the dance floor and away from Jamie, heading toward the car. At this point, she didn't need to fake sick, if she stayed any longer she would inevitably cause herself physical illness. On her way out, she took one glance back to see if Jamie saw her leaving. Of course he did, he hadn't taken his eyes off her since she got on the dance floor. All she could think was

that it was like driving past a car accident. You don't
want to look and you know there's a good chance you will
see something you aren't prepared to see, but you can't
look away. She disappeared with Will into the darkness of
the parking lot.

Fifteen

Threshold

The dust from the dirt road behind her was all she could see through the rear view mirror. Thankfully all the roads on the outskirts of town were dirt, so the inevitable dust-covered truck had never given anything away about where she had gone.

Will had left earlier that day to run some errands in the city and was swinging by Mike's afterword for a drink or two. Hailey wasn't expecting him home before nightfall and decided to take advantage of the free time to figure out, once and for all, what the hell she wanted. Her guilt for what she was doing to both men was wreaking havoc on her and since Will was the one who had no idea what was really going on, she remorsefully but gladly accepted the day to herself; even though she attempted to act slightly disappointed at the idea when he told her his days plans, she needed to sort things out with Jamie who she knew was in as much pain as she was. She waited 20 minutes after he left, just to make sure he hadn't randomly forgotten something and turned around for home again, then grabbed the keys to the truck and bolted, leaving the screen door swinging in the wind. Locking up wasn't even close to being on her radar at the moment.

Hailey had no sure way of knowing he would be there, but after their accidental run in at the wedding the night before, she knew she needed to see him and had a gut feeling he was thinking the same thing. It was Sunday so she couldn't exactly risk calling or writing to him in case Amy was within eyesight of his phone.

Even though the cabin was just over thirty minutes from her place, it seemed to take forever to get there. Hoping with everything she had in her that he had the same idea, she drove in a panic trying to think of some sort of game plan. Her mind raced back and forth, reliving every moment they had spent together and in turn, every moment she had spent with Will in between. This was all insane. It had gone too far and she knew she should walk away. On the other hand, it felt like things were just beginning and she had no idea if she could or even wanted to say goodbye to Jamie. She loved him. She loved them both, and she didn't know what that meant or what she should do about it. All she did know, was that hurting anyone wasn't part of the plan.

The long winding, single-lane dirt road that led to the cabin was like torture. It was their place, he had to be there. As she turned the last corner and the cabin came into view, she saw his truck parked out front and smoke coming from the chimney. Her heart was pounding. She didn't know what she was going to say or do, she just knew she had to see him and she hoped that somehow, her instincts would kick in and she would have all the answers. She had to make something right out of everything she felt she had made wrong the night before. For all the pain she had caused, knowingly and unknowingly.

Before she could even get the keys out of the ignition, she heard the front door open. She looked up to see Jamie walk out on the porch, looking as amazing as ever in his jeans, cowboy boots and a tucked in blue plaid shirt, the sleeves rolled up just a little. She jumped out of the truck and without a single thought, ran toward him. He quickly came down the two steps to the ground and grabbed her up in his arms, lifting her feet off the ground. With her arms around his neck, she didn't ever want to let go. The feeling of his strong body against hers, holding her so tightly and the smell of that cologne that got her every damn time, had made her decision for her. She couldn't end it, even if she wanted to. Tears started to run as she whispered "I'm sorry. I'm so so sorry."

"Darlin' don't be. You don't need to be," he said as he lowered her back onto her feet. He put his hands on either side of her face and gently held her. "You don't need to be sorry for anything."

"But the look on your face last night... I wasn't trying to hurt you. I wasn't, I swear. I saw you coming toward us and I panicked. I figured the only place we could avoid talking was the dance floor. Then I tried to leave and Will wanted one more dance. I..."

"I know. I wasn't mad at you. I promise. I knew you were just trying to get through the night, same as I was." With that, he leaned in and kissed her. It wasn't just any kiss though. It was a kiss of heartbreak and it felt like one of those moments when time stands still and you are able to memorize every tiny detail. How his lips met hers, partly open, warm and soft. How their noses just grazed eachothers and their bodies seemed to pull themselves together even closer than they had been before. It was like there was some kind of magic between them, like literal sparks flying. Yet it caused a painful ache in the core of Hailey's body, knowing that one day, it was very possible that she would have to experience the last time she would ever kiss this man or be held by him, and chances were, it wouldn't be a moment she would see coming.

Jamie bent down ever so slightly and scooped her up in his arms. Her legs over one arm, while his other held around her back. She reached around his neck and looked into his eyes as he carried her up the steps to the cabin.

"You know, you're supposed to marry a girl before you carry her over the threshold," she said; the sound of her voice sounding more like intent than simply stating a fact.

As he approached the door he paused. "We don't need a piece of paper to tell us how much this matters."

Nothing was more true than that. She had a piece of paper; they both did. Yet here they were, going against the vows they had made to other people, because they simply needed each other more than either could explain.

He stepped through the doorway of the cabin and just like that, the pain and despair that had been tearing her apart, left her and all she could feel was how severely she needed him. Instead of putting her down on her feet, Jamie carried her through the cabin past the small fire he had burning in the fireplace, to the bed. Everything was exactly as it had been the last time they were here. Untouched, as if the cabin had been waiting for them to come home.

He leaned over the bed, laying her down as close to the middle as he could. His arm never leaving her back. He laid down beside her, his other hand falling across her body and resting on her hip. Staring into his eyes, Hailey reached up and began undoing the buttons on his shirt. Starting with the top and working her way down slowly to his belt. She tugged on the bottom of the shirt, untucking it before undoing the last few buttons. She ran her hands up his chest and over his strong shoulders, moving his shirt out of the way as she went.

With her eyes locked on his; allowing him, almost begging him, to see her in her most vulnerable way, she once again lost herself completely in him.

Afterwards, instead of the usual rush to get back to their separate lives so no one noticed anything, they laid in each other's arms, trying to hold on as long as they could.

"I'm afraid I'm going to lose you," she said.

Knowing he had no words to comfort her, he held her a little tighter. "I know," he whispered. "I can't promise that we will be able to be together forever. I wish I could, but it's just not the hand we were dealt." He paused for a moment. "I can make one promise to you though. I promise you, that no matter what happens, or where we end up; this…" taking her hand, he placed it over his chest and held it there as if to put her hand on his heart. "…This is real, and always will be. Whether we are together or not, I promise you, I'm going to wake up each morning loving you until the day I die."

Looking into his eyes, she knew he meant every word he had said, and although she knew it should have brought her some sort of comfort, she realized the feeling of fear that had crept over her the night before had returned and was just as strong as it had ever been. The threat of losing him was becoming more and more real with each passing day and Hailey knew, neither one had any way of stopping it. They could put it off for as long as they were able and both knew they were willing to do that, but after last night it was painfully obvious to the both of them what the future held, regardless of whether they were able to stay together or not.

Jamie sat up and pulled his jeans on before walking over to the fireplace to toss another small log on, the way his grandfather would when something was bothering him. She watched him move about the room, unable to take her eyes off the look of his body in the glow of the fire. He was trying to keep her from seeing his pain by getting up and moving about the room, but she knew it was there, just as hers was. It was the entire reason he had a fire burning on a warm August day. She wrapped herself up in the quilt from the bed and made her way toward him.

"Do you have to get back right away?" he asked as she reached his side.

"No, I have a few hours."

"Hungry?"

Hailey nodded and Jamie kissed her on the forehead before heading toward the small kitchen to see what he could scrounge up for them. Since they had started coming to the cabin, they had been bringing small amounts of food to leave there, mostly canned food that would keep, for those rare moments they had a little extra time together. She turned back toward the fire and sat down on her knees in front of the stone fireplace, tucking the quilt underneath herself in order to protect from the firmness of the old wooden floor boards. She couldn't help but allow herself to be distracted by the flames flickering just a few feet away, becoming somewhat entranced by the way each flame seemed to disappear only to be brought back to life by the rest. Finally, glancing down at her hands on her lap she noticed her gold wedding band on her ring finger where it had always been. She hadn't taken it off since the day Will put it on her finger. Reaching for it she began to spin it around, almost as if each spin was a heads or tails choice.

"Chili's just heating up," Jamie said as he sat down behind Hailey, putting one leg on either side of her. He wrapped his arms around her shoulders and rested his cheek against hers.

Hailey reached up with one hand and placed it on his wrist as if to let him know she didn't want him to let go. "Were you waiting for me here?"

"Of course I was." His voice strong and assuring.

"But, how did you know I would come?"

"For the same reason you knew I'd be here."

She didn't know how she knew he would be there, she just did. Everything in her life felt like it was chaos and nothing seemed to make sense anymore, but somehow she knew he would be there waiting for her.

Hailey turned her body to face him, reaching up to feel the stubble on his face, she looked at each place her fingers grazed, taking in every inch of his skin. Letting the blanket slip down over her shoulders she reached for the button and zipper of his jeans, undoing them without taking her eyes from his. Still sitting on her knees, she lifted her legs to slip over his, sitting herself overtop of him. Leaning against the couch for support, Jamie slid his jeans off from underneath her and they made love in front of the warm fire.

Hailey left the cabin that day feeling emotionally exhausted and broken. She had gone there with the intent of figuring out what she truly wanted, but instead of leaving with an answer, she walked away with more confusion and questioning what was so utterly wrong with her that she couldn't make this choice! From the beginning, she knew this was going to be difficult, but she wasn't prepared for just how gut-wrenching it would actually be. Living two lives, feeling like two different people and loving two different men, for different reasons. It was enough to wreck someone.

Sixteen

Broken Promises

Will had been planning a boys weekend away with some of the guys from work for a few months. Sort of an end of summer celebration before they all got back to their regular teaching year and the opportunity had Hailey planning an attempted weekend with Jamie at the cabin. Although they hadn't worked out the kinks of how Jamie was going to get away without Amy thinking anything suspicious was up. Neither one of them liked the idea of saying he was with a friend, since in such a small town, there was a good chance she might bump into that friend or their wife and his story would be blown.

They had decided to try and hold off seeing each other during the week before their mini-vacation together to make sure they were caught up on life since they wanted to spend the time uninterrupted by work or worrying that they were falling behind. Hailey had to get caught up on her writing since she was dangerously close to missing a deadline and Jamie had been backlogged with clients since he kept sneaking off whenever he could to see her.

They were supposed to meet Saturday morning at the cabin. Jamie was going to head there Friday night ahead of her and Hailey would wait until Will left bright and early Saturday before packing and meeting him there around ten o'clock.

On the Wednesday morning before, Hailey's phone buzzed in her back pocket while she was getting Charlie's grain ready.

"This has been the longest week of my life and it's only Wednesday. Any chance you have some way of speeding things up a little? I need to see you."

"You are going to get us caught if you keep texting me like this you know! But yes, this week is moving in slow motion and I'm desperate to see you too."

"I know, I just couldn't help myself. I figured you were alone at this time of day anyway."

"Usually, but only because I'm in the barn. Don't forget, he's a teacher and it's still summer so he doesn't work as much. Summers off and all that!"

"Okay, I'll try to behave myself from now on. One last thing..."

She waited for him to finish that sentence.

"Don't bother packing too much in the way of clothing for this weekend. You won't need any of it if I have anything to do with it ;)"

A big smile crept across her face. Most of the time he was dead serious and super romantic, but every once in a while his playful and flirty side came through. It made her feel like they were teenagers falling in love.

"You see, I want to say something witty and make you think you'll need to work a little harder for it, but truth is, that sounds like the exact type of weekend I'm hoping for with you..."

"Good. Get there as early as you can. See you Saturday darlin'."

Hailey deleted the messages and slipped her phone back in her pocket, just in time for it to buzz one more time.

"Oh, just so you know, I told Amy I was taking Joe and doing a solo weekend camping trip to take a breather from the busy summer. She was a little put-off, but I told her I just needed a little time to myself. Can you bring Charlie? There's a bunch of trails around the property."

"So I guess I had better pack at least one outfit then?" she teased back.

"Just the one!"

Thursday afternoon Will came home from work just after three.

"Hey, Hails. Change of plans for the weekend babe," he called out to her from the driveway. She was bringing Charlie into the barn for dinner and when she heard what he said, her heart sank. There wasn't any way this was going to work out in her favour.

"What do you mean?" she asked with a puzzled and clearly upset look on her face.

"Don't look so disappointed!"

"Sorry, not disappointed at all. Just had hoped to get some uninterrupted writing done this weekend, that's all."

"Well how about you put that off and come with me instead? The guys had to back out and I can't get my deposit back, so I figured we might as well take advantage of a little together time. Ask what's her name down the road to handle things here for you like last time."

Hailey didn't go away very often, but on the one occasion she did, she had asked her neighbour to pop by each day and throw some hay and just make sure Charlie was alright.

Hailey opened her mouth to speak but stopped herself before she could actually say anything. She didn't know what to say. Every excuse she could think of didn't sound convincing. She finally settled on work. "I don't know Will. I mean, I really should be working. I'm going to miss my deadline if I don't find some time to get caught up."

"One weekend isn't going to make or break your book deal. I'm sure they'll give you an extension. They want the book, right? I doubt they'll toss the whole thing over a couple of days. Besides, you have all the time in the world, you're always here working away. How big is this book?"

There was the trap she had walked herself into. Yes, she should have her book done already, she was always supposed to just be here; as far as Will knew, she rarely went anywhere. But her life with Will was becoming one giant lie that was bound to catch up with her at some point. The truth was, she wasn't too far off from meeting her deadline since she had been playing catch-up all week, but she was quickly running out of excuses for why going on this trip wouldn't work out. The only thing she could think to tell him was that she just didn't want to go, but she knew it would just make him cancel and stay home on top of having his feelings hurt.

"Are you sure you want me to tag along? I mean, you've been looking forward to getting away for a long time. Might not be a bad thing to sit on the beach and enjoy some quiet," she said as she put Charlie in her stall.

Will walked up to her and wrapped his arms around her from behind, tucking his chin alongside her neck he said, "I also don't think it would be a bad thing for us to actually spend some time together. We haven't really been too focused on us this summer. I think we could probably use a little silence together." He sounded hopeful and happy and Hailey felt like the worst wife in the world. After all, there was still a huge part of her that was his; reality was, it was only that they had been together for so long at this point that they were sort of running on autopilot. Were they perfect together? Of course not, but she knew that no couple was.   He was right and she felt a twinge inside that he had noticed the space between them lately and wanted to reconnect with her. The other part of her, the part that belonged to Jamie, wanted to cry because now she had to cancel her weekend with him. It wasn't lost on her that she was literally about to have the exact same weekend plans, just not with the guy she had planned them with. Jamie was going to be livid.

"It sounds great," Hailey said, turning her head toward Will and smiling to try and assure him she was fully on board.

His arms slipped off her as he started to walk out of the barn. "Great. Maybe we can head out Friday instead and get a head start. I'll give them a shout and see if we can get the extra night."

Hailey smiled at him as he headed for the house. She grabbed Charlie's dinner and took it into her stall for her, trying to figure out how she was going to tell Jamie.

She figured she just had to rip the bandage so to speak and get it over with since she saw no way out of it. She grabbed her phone from her pocket and wrote.

"Are you busy?"

"Hey, no I have a few minutes." He wrote back almost instantly.

"Where are you? We have a problem with this weekend."

"I'm across town. What's the problem?"

"Will's friends cancelled and now he wants me to go away with him instead. I tried to tell him I had plans to write and a deadline to meet but he had every excuse for me to put it off and basically left me with no choice."

"Fuck. Are you kidding?"

"I know, I'm sorry. I will make it up to you, I swear!"

"Just tell him you don't want to go."

"I was going to but he would just cancel and stay home. Then I still couldn't get away." No sooner had she sent that text then she realized he probably saw that as the better option anyway. A weekend away at a cottage with another man, even if he was her husband, or staying put and living their routine way of life where nothing

really felt too overly special and where she might have a chance at sneaking off for an hour or so to see him.

"Can you get away Friday evening instead? Just for a few hours?" He was getting desperate.

"He wants to leave Friday to get a head start on the weekend."

Hailey knew he was angry but didn't know what to say to make it any better. They hadn't ever found an opportunity to spend a whole night together, let alone a weekend and she had literally just told him that she was cancelling with him to spend it with another man. Of course he was mad. It was five minutes before he wrote her back.

"It's not like I have any say in it anyway, so just let me know when it's my turn to see you."

"Jamie...." She was on the verge of tears realizing he wasn't just mad about the situation, he was mad at her for causing it. He had never been upset with her before and she found herself resenting Will for putting her in this position. *"I'm sorry, I don't know what you want me to do."*

There was an empty pail sitting on the floor beside Charlie's stall. Out of pure frustration, she kicked it to the other end of the barn. Charlie instantly stood up straight to find out what all the commotion was about, her ears perked forward and eyes darted toward the sound of the bucket rolling to a stop. Hailey yelled "fuck" while still holding her phone waiting for Jamie's answer. She walked over and picked up the bucket, and as she walked it back to where it came from, she realized it wasn't Will she needed to direct her anger at. He was just as wronged, even more than Jamie was and it was all at her own hand.

"Like I said, just let me know when it's my turn to see you," he repeated after about ten minutes. Short, to the point and refusing to let go of his anger. He was making a point and making it very clearly.

She didn't hear from him again and knew that no amount of grovelling right now was going to make things better or alleviate his anger. Maybe he had every right to be angry with her, she wasn't even sure anymore. At this point, she felt like there was some sort of ripple effect happening and everyone should be upset with her if they weren't already. She was starting to lose track of the pissed off who and what of wake Hailey.

Feeling like pretty much the worst person on the planet for the situation she had herself in and everything she was putting on both Jamie and Will, and for how much she had let Amanda down over the last few months, she stuffed her phone in her pocket, turned Charlie back out after her dinner and headed for the house. Will was in the shower when she got in and since they were supposed to leave the following day, she gave her neighbour a call to set things up, telling herself all she could do at this point was take things one moment and problem at a time.

Friday afternoon had Will acting more excited than Hailey had seen him in a while. She felt horribly guilty because she just couldn't find that level of happiness about getting away. A year ago, she would have been up early and packed and ready to go before Will could have even had time to open his eyes. A lot can change in a years time. She grabbed her computer hoping maybe she could sneak off and get some writing done, even though she knew that anyone would tell her she should be trying to focus on her obviously messed up marital situation. All she knew was she was feeling torn between two men and two different lives and had somehow messed them both up. It was starting to become obvious that eventually, it would come down to her having to make a choice but she didn't know how to do that. There just wasn't a right answer in any decision she could make. No matter what, someone she loved would get hurt and she would lose something and someone that she didn't know how to live without.

Hailey carried her bag out to the car where Will was waiting and tossed it in the trunk.

"Ready?" he asked as he went around to the driver's side and got in.

"Ya," Hailey said to herself, realizing that Will couldn't hear her now anyway since he was already in the car with the door closed. She couldn't help but notice the small differences between Will and Jamie. She had driven with Jamie enough to know that he never let her get to the truck door first. He always opened it for her. She couldn't remember a time when Will had done that. Jamie would have met her halfway when she walked out of the house and taken her bag for her, while Will had let her walk right past him to do it herself. It wasn't that she felt a man should have to do things like that for a women, and she honestly didn't think less of Will for not doing it, but the difference between the two men was startling. She liked that Will saw her as independent enough to not need to be taken care of; it had its own sense of romance in a way. With Jamie, it was just part of who he was. He was an old soul who did things in an older way and when she was with him she craved that feeling of stepping back in time where men courted women, held doors open for them and took them on picnic dates. And there it was, two different sides of her, each completed by two different men.

She knew she had put her feelings and relationship with Will on the backburner over the last little while and she needed to make up for it. With him, she was settled and they had already created a life together. Things were simple and she knew what to expect and how things were going to go. With Jamie, everything was new and they were just starting to find their way together. It was exciting and because they couldn't see each other often, the newness of it was lasting and admittedly, all-consuming.

Hailey and Will arrived at the cottage just before dinner that Friday afternoon. It had been a long time since they had gone away together and Hailey was trying desperately to muster up the right feelings to try and focus on the present and on Will.   She owed him that and so much more. She couldn't do anything about her relationship with Jamie while she was away anyway, so she tried to stuff him to the back of her mind, not that it was exactly an easy thing to do. There wasn't anything here to remind her of him and she hoped she might have a chance at just relaxing and ignoring her now reversed guilt. No matter which man she was with, she was wronging the other.

It was startlingly obvious as she watched Will light up talking about the cottage and what their weekend would entail that she had taken him for granted, assuming that as long as he didn't find out about Jamie, he would always just be there. She realized she simply hadn't paid attention to how little she had put into him and their life together. She hadn't stopped loving him, that was never the reason she was with Jamie. It wasn't a lacking in anything from Will. They just each had a different part of her. Regardless, she knew she had been neglecting things with Will, and she had decided to try and make the most of this weekend with him. It was the only thing she figured she had a chance at making better at the moment.

The cottage was bigger than what they needed since Will had booked it for four men, but it was quiet which Hailey found odd. She was so used to what she felt was the quiet farm life, but coming here she realized that real quiet happens when you step away from the dogs, chickens and horses. The quiet came from the stillness and the lack of actually having anything to do. However, the silence didn't do much to help distract her from the obvious so unfortunately, the out of sight out of mind idea was going to be a little tougher than she had expected. If the place was busy or at least had some sort of noise happening, she could maybe have something else to focus on.

The cottage had three bedrooms and a pullout couch in the living room with one decent size bathroom and an open concept kitchen and living room overlooking the beach. There was a fire pit in the sand, halfway between the cottage and the lake, and Hailey thought it would be a perfect place to spend the evening if you were looking to reconnect with someone or to find that 'something' that used to make everything else wash away.

After they brought their bags in and unpacked the groceries, Will grabbed the steaks and headed out to the BBQ just outside the kitchen on the deck. Hailey stayed inside, watching him through the patio doors, but for as much as she tried to stay focused on the present and give Will the attention he deserved, she couldn't get the thought of Jamie off her mind. Knowing he was upset with her was making her stomach turn. Did he go to the cabin without her? Was he at home with Amy? How upset was he? She decided to try and get a hold of him, in hopes of putting her mind at ease and being able to finally attempt making the most of her weekend.

"Hey, did you leave a rasp at my barn when you were there last?" Once again, texting him a random question to not give anything away.

"Sure didn't."

Her heart sank with his short response and she knew that he was clearly still furious with her. Before she could figure out what to say, her phone buzzed again.

"I'm at the cabin, receptions not great."

Clearly he wasn't too interested in talking to her, giving himself an out before she even started. She thought she would have felt relief to hear from him, but she didn't feel better, the guilty feeling in the pit of her stomach was getting worse.

"You went to the cabin anyway?" she asked, trying to ignore his anger.

"Ya. I wasn't in the mood to stick around home and be asked why I was upset or why I cancelled my plans."

"Jamie I meant it when I told you I loved you. I haven't ever doubted that. I'm just so sorry for all of this. I honestly didn't see this coming and I just had no way out of it."

"Don't worry about it. We can't have everything when we're going about things the way we are."

The knot in her stomach tightened and suddenly she realized, she wasn't entirely sure if he was staying with Amy because he wanted to, or if it was because she was staying with Will. They hadn't actually talked about it. The last time the idea had come up was the day they confessed how they felt about each other and Hailey had said she couldn't leave Will. Jamie hadn't said what he was or wasn't willing to do to be with her, aside from accepting that she wasn't leaving her husband.

"Can I see you when I get back?" She knew they had a lot to talk about but she didn't want to do it through texts.

"We'll figure something out. Text me Wednesday. I should be out a little closer your way that afternoon."

"I don't mind driving to see you. Can we figure something out for Monday? I don't know if I can wait until Wednesday." She was terrified to think that he could have waited that long and to feel like he was talking to her the way he used to, before they had any kind of connection at all. Back when she didn't matter to him.

"Give me a shout Monday morning and I'll figure something out."

Realizing he was done with the conversation and wasn't going to go any easier on her at the moment, she decided to let it go. *"I love you,"* she wrote, hoping he would at least be able to say it back.

"I love you too."

Since they had started seeing each other, he hadn't been this short with her, nor had he ever purposely tried to make her feel bad which is what she assumed he had been attempting to do. For a moment, all she wanted to do was ignore both men and spend a week at the farm with Charlie and her writing and not be bothered. The thought that maybe the both of them were also better off in that scenario crossed her mind.

She deleted the messages, tucked her phone in the back pocket of her jean shorts, took a deep breath and headed out on the deck with Will.

"Everything okay?" he asked.

Trying to shake the obvious look of sadness from her face, she lied and said "Ya, just checking to make sure everything is okay with Charlie." With that, Hailey walked toward Will and wrapped her arms around him from behind. It had been a long time since she initiated any closeness between them and he seemed to notice the change. He turned in her arms, now facing her, he pulled her in close and kissed the top of her head.

"I'm glad the guys cancelled. We needed this," he said, still holding her close with his chin resting on top of her head.

"I'm sorry, I've been preoccupied with my book lately. I've been a pretty poor excuse for a wife."

"Well, you're not the only one who's been busy. We always find our way Hails."

After dinner, Hailey wandered out to the firepit on the beach. There was already a good amount of kindling and firewood stacked off to the side and she had brought some newspaper and matches down with her and got to work starting a fire. Not long after it was going, Will came down with a bag of marshmallows, a cooler and some blankets. Laying the blankets out in the sand, he set the cooler off to the side, opened it and grabbed a beer for each of them. The breeze off the water was warm, but the extra blankets were welcome the later in the evening it got. They roasted marshmallows and had a few drinks, physically soaking up the time together, but they didn't talk much and Hailey wondered why. Things between

them had seemed to get off to a good start this weekend,
but the silence seemed to be too much of their norm lately
to be changed. They used to stay up late all the time,
talking about future plans and dreams. Maybe they had
reached them all already she thought, and now they were
just living them. The idea made her sad.

For a weekend that was meant to bring the
romance back into their lives and give them an
opportunity to reconnect, Hailey kept finding that each
attempt felt mildly more forced than the last. Old habits
were still there and as strong as ever. They fell into their
same old routine of quiet talk and spending short bits of
time together, but somehow mostly going about their own
business. Even though Will had begged her to come with
him, saying the time together was exactly what they
needed, he woke up Saturday morning and the first thing
he did was grab a book and a coffee and head to the deck
to read. It wasn't exactly a together activity, nor was it
out of the norm of how their relationship had become.
She knew he simply saw it as a moment to relax and
would be confused if she brought up the point that it sort
of went against the idea of reconnecting.
When Hailey laid down in bed that night, Will put
his book down on the nightstand and rolled toward her.
She knew this meant he wanted to have sex. He never
put his book down or rolled toward her if that wasn't his
intention and the longer they were married, the less often
it happened. It had been months since they had been
together in this way and she wasn't sure how she felt
about it. They hadn't actually had sex since she started
seeing Jamie and the more she thought about it, she
realized that this part of her had become more of

something she shared with him, vs her own husband. She suddenly felt like she would be cheating on Jamie by sleeping with Will.

There was no desperation, no attempt at passion or the feeling of needing each other so badly they couldn't breath without being together. There was however, tenderness and caring and knowledge of what worked for each other, but the act itself felt more about the finish line so to speak, than craving all the in between touches and moments, as if those things had been exhausted years ago. Hailey found herself laying underneath a man she had promised herself to, hoping they would both finish quickly so it could be done with. It wasn't bad sex, it was just sex and nothing more.

When they were through, Hailey rolled over, turning her back to Will.

"Goodnight," she whispered, as quiet tears fell from her eyes landing on her pillow.

"Night babe," he said, and without noticing anything was wrong, he picked up his book and turned his reading light back on.

Hailey wondered if she had never met Jamie, would she have ever noticed how mundane and practiced her sex life with Will had become? She supposed with any couple, things sort of fall into a routine, but to be able to go so long without feeling that need for such a desperate connection and to not want more from each other than just the act itself, just felt wrong now. They were losing each other but she felt like she was the only one noticing.

They slept in the next morning, taking full advantage of the idea of a mini-vacation. As the morning light began to filter in the room, Hailey opened her eyes. The sight of Will sleeping next to her caught her off guard.

She hadn't taken much time to really see him lately and she knew it was because she had herself wrapped up in Jamie and trying to find time with him, but it also had to do with her guilt. To really look at Will hurt her, and she knew if he ever noticed her in those moments, she would break. Watching him while he slept was the first time she really felt like she could take him in and face the truth of what she had done, without actually causing him pain. His unshaven face was as handsome as she had always remembered. There was no denying she was still very much attracted to him and she loved the sense of romance and how safe it made her feel to be laying next to a slightly older man. It crossed her mind to reach over and wake him with a passionate kiss or a suggestive touch but she didn't know if he would react the way she hoped, and she was afraid if he didn't, it would crush her. She wanted them to fall in love all over again, maybe prove to her that he was where she was supposed to be and that what she had with Jamie was a temporary bandage to a rough patch in their marriage. She wanted an easy answer to an impossible situation, even though she knew what she had built with Jamie was somehow just as much a part of her as what she had with Will. She was torn.

As Will began to stir in his sleep, Hailey slipped out of bed, grabbed a blanket and headed to the beach to sit and take in the sound of the water and the feeling of sand between her toes. The weekend hadn't really done what she had hoped it would. If anything it had caused her to be even more confused than before she left. She wondered if somehow Will felt like they had reconnected or if he was beginning to acknowledge that everything was still the same?

"Hails, you coming up? We have to get packed and out of here in the next two hours."

Looking back to the deck where Will was standing, she nodded. "Be right there." She stood up, shook the sand off herself and the blanket and headed back up to pack.

Monday morning had Will running late for work which wasn't a great start to the new school year. The weekend away had perhaps relaxed him just a little too much and he was carrying that through into the week. Hailey did her best to help him with the little things, like making sure his keys and coffee were ready at the door to go and packing him something to eat during the day. He normally bought his lunch when he was at work, but Hailey thought she'd attempt to go a little above and beyond for him since she had taken him for granted so much lately. Maybe if she put in more effort, he would feel it and be more responsive to her. She was starting to question whether that's truly what she wanted anymore, but she knew she owed it to him to try. She would have to keep it to herself though. It would break Jamie's heart to know she was trying to make an effort in her marriage.

She kissed Will goodbye and headed to the barn for chores before grabbing a quick shower. By the time she was dressed and ready for her day, it was already nine thirty. She grabbed her phone to text Jamie. Breaking every rule they had come up with on how to get in touch with each other without getting caught, she texted him a point-blank message and kept her fingers crossed that he wasn't sitting around with Amy randomly on a regular work day. *"Can I come see you today? I know you probably don't have much time."*

With her phone in her hand, she grabbed her coffee and headed for the porch swing. Time waiting for his response went by slower than she could bear. Each minute seemed to pass at the rate of five. Watching Charlie graze in the field helped to keep her somewhat occupied but not enough to fully distract her from knowing the conversation they were going to need to have when he had a few minutes.

"I switched my Wednesday with today. I'm twenty minutes from your place. Are you alone? I'll come to you."

The knot in her stomach came back.

"Ya, I'm alone until 6. When can you come?"

"On my way now."

Hailey was still sitting on the porch swing when Jamie pulled in. He got out of the truck, walked up onto the porch and leaned against the railing across from her. Her heart sank a little that he didn't come near her. They always kissed each other hello at the very least. He was either still fuming mad or he knew just as much as she did that they needed to talk and clear the air.

"I think we need to talk. Or, at least I do. I don't know. We haven't really spoken about a few things. Mainly, what you are actually wanting," she said.

His gaze went from her eyes to the field and it felt like forever before he spoke.

"I know. I just don't have any answers," he said, looking back toward her. Suddenly his voice became stern and he stood up. "I don't know how to talk about what I want, because I can't have it. I'm sitting on the sidelines watching someone else scoop you up from me over and over again and it takes everything I have in me not to do something about it, because I'm not allowed to. I know I can't have all of you..."

"No, Jamie, you can't! And I can't have all of you. If you've forgotten, I'm not the only one who's married to someone else here," she interrupted. She found herself angry with him at the insinuation that he just sat around all the time waiting for her to be free for him. She knew that this past weekend had centered on her dropping her plans with him for her husband, but she couldn't let him forget that he had a wife, and at one point, he would probably have to do the same to her. "Do you think it's been easy for me to know that each time you leave me, you go home to your wife? Do you think I don't cringe and find myself sick to my stomach knowing what you go home to do with her? It makes me want to scream to know you kiss and hug her, that you have sex with her! Most days it makes me want to break everything in sight! I have no right to feel anything about it because I'm the one in the wrong here, but I can't help it because I fell in love with you. But the one thing I haven't done, is make you feel bad for it like you did to me this weekend. I know you don't want to hear it, but until this weekend, I haven't slept with my husband, nor has he even so much as seen me without my clothes on since you and I started all of this and I'm going to guess that you can't say the same thing about you and your wife." With her accusation, tears began to stream down her face and she stopped talking to try and collect herself. Her heart broke when his silence told her she was right. "And when I did sleep with him this weekend, my own husband, the entire time I felt like I was cheating on you and it broke me. The whole time I was begging for it to be over." She waited for him to yell back at her or storm off to his truck and leave. After all, it's how things would have gone if the argument was with Will. But instead, he paced back and forth and finally stopped at the railing facing the field.

With his back turned to her he finally said "You're right. I know. I didn't have any right to be upset. I chose this as much as you did, knowing exactly what I was getting myself into." He turned and walked over to where she was sitting. As he crouched down in front of her, he took her hands in his. "Hailey, I just can't stand the thought of him having a part of you at all. I get it and I know I have to accept it, but I don't like it. I'm sorry I let you feel it, it's just been a lot lately I guess and I didn't handle it well."

She focused on the warmth of his hands holding hers, letting her anger settle.   "First seeing us together at the wedding, dancing together and then me cancelling plans with you to spend the weekend with him."

"Ya it's just been a lot to swallow." He squeezed her hands a little with his. "I know that he's a part of who you are and I don't have any right to make you feel bad for that. I guess, I just want to be selfish with you and keep you for myself."

"Jamie," she said, afraid to ask him what she needed to ask. His eyes looked up from their hands and she took a deep breath. "Maybe I don't have any right to ask you this, but I realized something while I was away this weekend. When we first told each other how we felt...about us, I told you I couldn't leave Will." She paused for a moment. "But you didn't say you couldn't leave Amy." The words seemed to fall from her lips without her being ready and the fear she felt inside seemed to grow with anticipation of what he would say.

She couldn't even imagine what she wanted his answer to be.

"My marriage isn't what yours is," he said. "I've come to realize that over the last year. It's nothing bad, it just isn't something great either. It just is what it is and had I not met you, I probably wouldn't think anything of it." As he spoke he stood up and backed away toward the railing again, almost as if to protect Hailey from hearing him talk about his wife.

Hailey stood up and took a few steps toward him, in part to show him he didn't ever need to keep distant from her for any reason and because she needed him in this moment. She needed to know that they had each other no matter what. "If I asked you to leave her, would you?"

Turning his head to the left and looking slightly over his shoulder, but without having to come face to face he asked, "Is that what you want me to do?"

Hailey realized his truth in that moment; she knew his answer without him having to say it. He would leave his wife if she asked, he would do anything for her. The only reason he was staying with Amy was for comfort in the moments he couldn't be with Hailey. To know that she was with her husband and have to go home alone would be too much to bear. She choked back the answer she wanted to give him and wiped the tears from her eyes that were beginning to build again.

"No," she finally said. "No, I won't ask you to leave your wife." She couldn't bring herself to say she didn't want to ask him to leave, because the reality was, she very much did want to ask him to leave her. She did want him all to herself and to know that when he left her each time, he wasn't going to the arms of another woman. But she loved him too much to deny him something that she herself wasn't willing to give up.

Neither one had any desire to say much more than they already had. They had managed to hurt each other yet need each other equally as much all in a half hour time frame. Hailey knew he would be leaving soon and couldn't bear the thought of it ending this way, so she took a chance that he wouldn't push her away, and walked up behind him, wrapping her arms around his chest and laying her cheek against his back. She felt his chest rise and lower as he took a deep breath and let it out with a sigh of what she hoped was relief, and placed his hands over her hers. After a few moments he turned in her arms to face her.

"I have to get going, but I want to see you soon. Can we do that?" he asked.

"Of course," she said with a slight smile, looking up at him.

"Okay, good." The look on his face was one of fear; fear of hurting her, that he had hurt her already, fear of losing her and fear of living the rest of his life caught in the middle of those feelings. "Can I kiss you?" he asked, while still in the midst of the nervous embrace they had been holding.

"Jamie," she said, as if to let him know he never had to ask her permission to kiss her.

She reached up and placed her hands on either side of his face, letting her fingers find their way around to the back of his neck and pulled him ever so slightly towards her. He leaned down and kissed her gently. It was once again, one of those kisses that makes time stop, not for how passionate it was, although it was passionate, but for the longing they both felt behind it. In that moment, Hailey had made a conscious decision to commit to memory every touch, every pause, every detail of how his lips felt against hers and the way in which he kissed her. How the back of his neck felt under her fingertips and how his hands seemed to find their home on her lower back, of the warmth of his body and how the smell of him was intoxicating.

He walked down the few steps of the front porch and headed toward his truck, pausing as he reached the driver's side door. He turned to look at Hailey, who had moved toward the steps and held her arms crossed in front of her chest.
"I love you," he said, still with a look of fear on his face.
"I love you too Jamie. More than you know." Somehow she always felt like she was on the verge of losing him.

Seventeen

Baby Talk

Over the next few weeks, Hailey and Jamie weren't able to see each other more than twice. Both times had felt as though they were trying to repair something that had been broken.

The first time they met, it was a quick few moments between Jamie's clients, pulled over on a side road somewhere on the outskirts of town. Hailey had made him lunch and brought it out to him and they sat in his truck while he ate. For the first time, conversation didn't come easily to them, as neither really knew what to say. They had such little time together lately, that talking about how hard this all was felt like a waste of time. Pretending that there wasn't a lot of strain on them wasn't an option either, because they both knew how heavily it was weighing on them. It was just something they would have to endure and hope would pass. They chatted a little about work and her writing, and avoided anything that had to do with Amy, Will or Amanda's wedding.

The second time they were able to meet up, they both had more time and made their way to the cabin. Hailey had gotten there first and was sitting on the front porch waiting when Jamie pulled in the laneway. Since the cabin was a place they rarely did much talking anyway, Jamie wasted no time in scooping Hailey up off the steps, carrying her inside and setting her down on her feet next to the bed. Pushing her against the wall with a little more force than she was used to him showing, she fully let go of any fear about their relationship and gave into how desperately they needed each other and how much they had missed each other. It was all she could do not to physically rip the buttons of his shirt to get it off of him. She wanted him to own her and to make her feel all the strength he had in his body. Stumbling and falling backwards on the bed, she dug her fingers into his back as he pushed against her, begging him to be closer, yet there was no space between them. The actual act didn't last that long but left them both out of breath and visibly worked. As Jamie collapsed on the bed beside Hailey, breathing heavily and warm with sweat, she turned her head to face him and couldn't help but smile as their eyes met. They had made love to each other in that cabin dozens of times before, but never before had it been so primal. It was as if they had taken all the fear and pain they had been going through and bottled it up, releasing it in their need for each other.

As Hailey was getting dressed to leave, Jamie asked if she thought she would be able to sneak off for a few hours this weekend. Although she desperately wanted to, she made a decision to keep a secret from Jamie. She had never lied to him before, but with everything they had been going through, she couldn't bear the thought of hurting him anymore. Her wedding anniversary with Will was coming up on the weekend and she knew that if she told him it would only cause him pain.

She told him that she didn't think it would be possible but would call him if she'd be able to manage a little time away. It broke her heart to see the look of hope on his face. She pulled her boots on and kissed him deeply before saying goodbye and leaving that day. Tears flowed down her cheeks as she drove home, the guilt of lying to Jamie almost more than she could bear.

Hailey could hear Will rummaging around the kitchen and since it was their anniversary, she assumed he was trying to surprise her with breakfast, which was out of the norm, but she wasn't going to complain if that was really what he was up to. She welcomed the idea and the chance to stay in bed a little longer and soak in the morning light that was now filling the room. The sun that streaked in through the window felt warm on her skin and she opened her eyes to see the leaves slowly falling and swirling around the yard as the wind blew ever so slightly. Fall was, after all, her favourite time of year and waking up this way just put her in a good mood.

"Happy Anniversary!" Will said as he pushed the bedroom door open with his shoulder. He was carrying a wooden tray with breakfast for two.

Hailey smiled and sat up in bed, pulling the pillows up behind her back to lean on. "Happy Anniversary."

Will placed the tray over her lap and leaned over it to kiss her on the forehead before sitting down on the edge of the bed. A small mason jar with fresh picked wild daisy's was placed between the coffee mugs.

"You must have been up early to get all this done. Thank you, this is...wonderful." She let the word sort of linger as she needed a minute to appreciate the thoughtfulness of it all herself. It wasn't like him to plan anything for their anniversary and she wondered what had made him think to do all of this. Looking down at the tray, she couldn't believe she would have ever entertained the idea of someone else. In this moment it was clear as day that she loved Will and always had. Unable to take her eyes off him, she smiled and felt herself take a deep breath. She allowed her love for him to come flooding through her like the morning light shining into the room.

"This is more than wonderful," she said smiling. "It's perfect."

They ate breakfast together in bed and reminisced about their wedding day. When they were done, Will took the tray and set it on the top of the dresser. He crawled back into bed, laying down on top of the covers next to Hailey. "So I've been thinking..." he started.

Hailey looked at him puzzled. "You have, have you? What about?"

"I think we should have a baby." The words came out with absolute confidence and certainty that the idea would be met with excitement.

Hailey, on the other hand, felt like the wind had been knocked out of her. She had always wanted to be a mother and in the first few years of their relationship she had been ready to start a family with Will. But now, things were different. She still wanted to be a mother and felt the need as deeply as she had ever felt it, but she knew things in her life were a mess, caught between two men she loved and then adding an innocent child to the situation felt like a twist she couldn't wrap her mind around. Instantly, she jumped to the thought of telling Jamie she was going to have a baby with Will and then back to the thought of telling Will she wasn't ready. Neither man would believe she was actually committed to the answer she gave them.

"A baby. You want to have a baby?" she asked, trying to keep from looking utterly confused and unsure of what to do or say.

"Yea, I'm finally at a place at the college where I can look at freeing up a little more time without risking anything and you're all set here with the farm and your writing. I just think it's the right time for us to start thinking about it."

Never in a million years did she think she would ever be so torn when the man she loved and was married to, asked her if she was ready to have a baby with him. Without knowing how to react, she simply wrapped her arms around Will and hugged him tightly. Thankful that in order to even consider having a baby she would need to stop her birth control and that was something that would take time. She didn't have to figure this out now. She just hugged him and decided to try and enjoy their weekend together, hoping he wouldn't bring it up again until after she had some time to figure out what she really wanted to do.

Hailey sat on the front porch swing after Will left for work Monday morning. She had made a coffee, but couldn't stomach it and left it sitting on the kitchen counter. Her heart was pounding and she could feel that cold feeling creeping down her spine that you feel moments before you pass out. She didn't think she would actually faint, but it was highly likely that the stress of this day would make her throw up. She picked up her phone and decided to just rip the bandage off, which seemed to be somewhat of a theme in her life these days.

"Charlie blew a shoe. Can you fit us in today?" She knew she would probably reach him before he started his day and should get back to her pretty quickly.

"I'm crazy busy today, too bad she didn't lose it yesterday. I'll see what time I'm done here and let you know. We'll make it work sometime today. As long as it's before 6?"

The hope he had in seeing her was almost enough to make her sick right then and there. He had no idea what was coming. She couldn't stand that after everything they had just gone through, after lying to him the week before in an attempt to spare his feelings, she now had to break the news to him that her husband wanted to have a baby with her.

"I'm so sorry I didn't get a chance to get away this weekend. There wasn't any way I could have snuck off without being questioned." It wasn't a lie, at least that's what she told herself. Truthfully, she would have been grilled if she had tried to leave on their anniversary, but Jamie didn't need to know the real reason why.

"But ya, I'm here alone until about 6 tonight." She thought about telling him they needed to talk, but decided against it in hopes of not ruining his entire day.

"K, I should be able to get out of here in a few hours. You might have to meet me though."

"Ok." She couldn't bear to keep the conversation going any longer. How could she make small talk with him, or even fake being happy and pleasant when she was about to deliver this blow. He would be angry and hurt but would feel betrayed again if she pretended nothing was up now.

He called her around noon and said he could meet her out near the old railway trail. He only had a short time between his clients but said it was worth it to see her. Guilt-ridden, she got in the truck knowing this wasn't something she could avoid. She hadn't actually told Will she was ready or willing to have a baby with him, but she hadn't said no either.

She turned left onto a road she wasn't familiar with and drove slowly enough that she could keep her eye out for an entrance to the old hiking trail. She was about two minutes down the road before she finally saw it and pulled in right behind Jamie. He was already outside, leaning against the side of his truck waiting for her.

She opened the door, got out and started to walk toward him. Realizing she couldn't look at him, she knew she had made her decision. This moment was going to break them and she knew it.

"What's wrong?" he asked, standing up straight and turning to face her. He knew her too well to not notice that something was terribly wrong.

Tears started to well up in her eyes and as she took a final step toward him, she looked up, but over his shoulder and then turned away, looking into the woods.

"What is it?" fearing Will had found out about them or worse, that she wanted to end things, Jamie began to panic. "Hailey…"

"Please don't hate me," she whispered.

"Hailey, what's going on?"

"Will wants…" she felt her throat closing in. She coughed and began again. "Will wants to have a baby."

Dead silence. They both knew why she was telling him. If she was against the idea, she would have just told Will she wasn't ready and there wouldn't have been anything for her to tell Jamie.

His skin felt like it was on fire, his blood boiling with anger at the realization that no matter how much of her heart he had, he would never have all of it. He hated that he had to share her and somewhere deep inside he knew that one day it would have to end, but he hadn't considered that he might actually lose her so soon. He wanted to tell her to say no and keep things going the way they were or even beg her to leave Will and be with him fully, but he knew he couldn't. He loved her too much to deny her the chance to be a mother and he knew that if he put up any kind of a fight over this, it would just end up hurting her more than she already was and he couldn't stand the thought. He had already made that mistake once and he wouldn't make it again.

His silence was terrifying to her and made her feel even more sick to her stomach than she had on the drive there. She needed him to say something, anything at all.

He turned away from her and toward his truck, putting his hands on the hood he leaned into it. With his back turned to her, she was finally able to look up at him, but before she could say anything, he smashed his fists into his truck. The sound of the force of his hands smashing into the hood's metal rang through the woods. She jumped at the sound. She had never seen him so angry and truth be told it scared her to death. She began to cry.

"I'm sorry," she whispered through her tears.

Hearing her cry made him turn around. He needed to hold her and fix this for her, even if he didn't really know how to and even if it meant he had to give her up.

"Hailey," he said as he turned and walked toward her. He reached out and wrapped her up in his arms. "Darlin you're shakin'."

She loved when he called her that but the fear that it would be the last time she heard him say it made her feel like she was experiencing a death. Her heart was breaking.

"Ask me not to. Please, just tell me not to," she sobbed. "I don't know what to do."

"Listen to me." He pulled away from her slightly so he could tell her face to face, but didn't let go of her completely. "Yes you do. It's ok. I'm not worth giving up having a child. You are going to make an amazing mother, I know you will and I'm not going to stand here in your way." He wasn't sure how he was even getting these words out because for as much as he wanted to believe he was able to let her go, he was raging inside. "I love you and I've had my chance at being selfish with you. We both know that this is something you want." His voice trailed off for a moment. "You wouldn't be here right now if it wasn't." He paused again, hoping he wasn't hurting her by saying the truth. "I'm going to remember every detail of us for the rest of my life, but we both knew this wasn't going to be able to last. Not for a lack of wanting it to, god knows this isn't one of those things that just fades." He paused again, allowing the thought that he would always love her to overwhelm him. "Had we met first, I'd be the one asking you to have a baby..."

Hearing him speak those words wrecked her. She covered her face with her hands, unable to control her crying. She couldn't breath and her knees became weak like she was going to collapse. He was letting her go and she felt like she was dying.

"Hailey," he said as she began to pull away from him. His own heart was shattering but he had to hold it together for her. He knew she loved him, but he also knew she had never fallen out of love with Will, despite their struggles. That wasn't why she was with him. Jamie knew he just somehow found a part of her she didn't even know existed until him and that part of her would always be his whether they were together or not. He never expected she would walk away from something that had fit with her for so long, no matter how much she loved him.

Hailey took a few steps back and turned toward her truck, putting her hands out to brace herself against it. Closing her eyes she took a deep breath, replaying his words in her head so she could always remember exactly what he said and the way he said it. *Had we met first, I'd be the one asking you to have a baby..."* Another deep breath. She stood up straight and wiped the tears from her face. Collecting herself, she turned to face him and for the first time that day, their eyes met. He was broken, she could see it. The kind of broken that a man doesn't recover from and it would forever be her fault.

"I love you," she said, holding back the flood of tears she knew was just on the brink of crashing down on her.

"I love you too."

With that, she turned away and got in her truck to leave, going against everything in her screaming not to. She couldn't even bring herself to touch him again. A clean break, she had no choice. For her sake and his. She hoped he would find enough anger in this to hate her. It was the only way she thought he might be able to move on, but deep down, she knew he would never be able to. He could have fought for her but instead, chose her over himself. If that wasn't a true act of love, to let her go, then she didn't know what was.

The memory of backing out of that narrow dirt road, watching Jamie standing beside his truck, not able to take his eyes off of her was burned into her memory. She had never experienced pain like she did that day and she didn't think she would experience anything like it again.

Hailey had found another farrier to take Jamies place but she had no desire to really get to know him past his name and when their appointment was. She had stayed in the barn for the first few trims but had finally asked if he was comfortable being left to do his work while she did hers around the farm.

Will had followed through with his idea of backing away from work a little so he could be around more often and had really taken to the thought that they were working on building a family together. She had never really envisioned him this way, the doting Dad to be, but it suited him and she found a sense of peace in that.

Six months after she had said goodbye to Jamie, she found herself standing in the bathroom, staring at a pregnancy test waiting the full three minutes it suggested before reading the results. She hadn't told Will she thought she was pregnant and for as much as she did want to have a baby with him, she knew that a positive on that test made the end of her and Jamie final. She had finally agreed to start trying a month or so after Will initially brought up the idea, but for one reason or another, this wasn't coming easily to them. Hailey assumed that the heartache she was going through was probably a major reason why her body just hadn't been cooperating.

The timer on her phone went off. Three minutes was up. Completely at a loss for what result she needed to see, she turned the test over. Her heart sank and with it, her ability to stand up. She crumbled to the floor as tears rolled down her cheeks. Ten minutes went by before she could get herself up. She walked to the mirror and wiped what was left of her tears away. She picked the test up off the bathroom floor and opened the door, taking a deep breath she walked down the hall to the living room where Will was sitting with the dogs. One look at her and he knew. He jumped up off the couch, smiling as big as she figured he possibly could. "Are you sure!?"

Hailey held out the test, showing him the very clear positive result. His love for this moment was infectious and for a split second she allowed herself to forget that a part of her was grieving a loss that would never heal.

Will ran over and scooped her up in his arms, spinning her around the room. When he finally set her back down on her feet, he got down on one knee and holding her hips, he kissed her belly. It was the second time she felt that movie magic moment in their lives and she couldn't help but smile.

Hailey had spent the next few months trying to come to grips with the idea that she would never again feel Jamie's touch. She told herself daily that she had made the right choice and that her grief was somehow justified for the pain she had caused him and the pain it would cause Will to find out what she had done behind his back. Her torture was her karma. Yet every once in a while, she found herself in a day dream, that it was Jamie she was waiting at home for each day and that the baby she was carrying was his. In those moments she felt settled and happy. But Will would be the one to come home to her and she found herself needing to make a point each day to make note of what she loved about him and their life together. She was beginning to feel lost in her own world and by the time she was in her second trimester, she was questioning whether she had made a mistake. She knew she had made many, but which one had gotten her here?
She didn't want to hurt Will and knew if he found out he would be utterly crushed. So she exaggerated her happiness and excitement over everything. She couldn't let him see that she was simply going through the motions and she told herself that eventually, it would all come together. Eventually she would truly feel that way, that she just needed to get past her grief and guilt and one day she would be truly at peace. Will and their baby deserved that and she would find a way to give that to them.

Eighteen

The Gift

Hailey looked down at her feet and smiled at what was starting to get in the way of her view. Putting her hands on her growing belly, she spoke to her unborn baby, telling him or her how much she already loved them and how excited she was for them to arrive. She clung to the excitement of becoming a mother and more often than not, allowed herself to forget the world around that. The baby became her only real happiness.

She was already four months along, but they had decided they didn't want to know the sex of the baby until it was born.

Will had made sure the nursery was all set with a crib, change table and rocking chair and wouldn't let Hailey lift a finger but to pick out bedding, decorations and clothes. He was taking over a lot of the farm chores on top of his teaching schedule and made sure to call home every night before he left work to see if she needed anything. She didn't exactly love that she was essentially just sitting and having everything done for her, but she knew that it was just Will's way of showing how much he cared. She got out for her daily walk and brought the animals treats to keep herself busy while Will was at work and spent the rest of her time working on a new book. She wouldn't tell Will what it was about, but would spend hours locked away writing. She had needed to find an outlet for her pain when she had parted ways with Jamie and so she wrote. She wrote their love story and what she imagined it would have been had she made the other choice that day in the woods. A few times since then, she had found herself driving out past the cabin, never pulling into the driveway, but just slowing down enough to see a quick glimpse of it. She often wondered if he still went there but was thankful his truck hadn't been there when she was. Her goal had been to finish her book before the baby was born and publish it under a pen name. She supposed she hoped one day he might read it and know it was their story and know that it meant everything to her, but putting her own name on it was putting them both at risk. She knew this story held too much truth and couldn't risk it being read by Will or anyone who would put the pieces together. The book was her way of finding closure, at least she hoped it would guide her there and help her close the door to the past.

After spending most of the morning tucked away writing, Hailey realized she had spent too much time thinking about Jamie for one day and decided to wander out to the field to see Charlie. She needed the fresh air and even though it was June, thankfully it hadn't gotten too hot outside yet. She grabbed a few carrots from the fridge and stepped out onto the front porch, nearly tripping over a gift bag. It wasn't there when Will left for work this morning and she hadn't heard anyone knocking so she assumed Will had left it for her as a surprise. She picked it up and brought it into the kitchen, setting the carrots down on the counter beside the bag. There wasn't a card, just a plain brown paper gift bag with white tissue paper inside. She reached in and pulled out the tissue, surprised at how heavy it was. Unwrapping the paper she suddenly realized this wasn't from Will at all. Staring in shock at a pony-sized horseshoe, hand made into a dreamcatcher, she knew exactly who had left this on her doorstep. In that moment, she knew the door to the past would never be closed. She ran out the door and down the porch steps, stopping once her feet hit the dirt of the laneway. Looking as far to the end as she possibly could, she hoped that he was still there somewhere. When she realized he was long gone, she held the gift close to her chest, closed her eyes and as a single tear fell she whispered, "Jamie."

How had he shown up to her door and not let her know he was there? Maybe he was trying to protect her or maybe he thought it was just too much for him to bear, but she knew there was only one place he would be now and she had to go see him.

After grabbing her keys and getting in the truck, she stretched the seatbelt out around her growing belly, clicking it in place. Turning the ignition, she glanced over at the dreamcatcher laying on the passenger seat. She felt a flood of emotions wash over her and realized she was probably making a really big mistake going to see him but she couldn't stop herself.

She knew he was there before she even turned into the laneway. It had been raining almost non stop for days and she could see tire tracks in the mud leading down the dead end road. No one ever went there but the two of them so she knew he was there. She turned in and braced herself for the moment she saw him again, not knowing how this would turn out but at the very least, she wanted to thank him in person. She knew he had made that gift himself and it meant more to her than she would ever be able to put into words. As she pulled up to the cabin, she saw his truck and parked behind him, nervously undoing her seat belt. He had to have heard her pull in and she hoped he would come out rather than her having to knock. She wasn't sure she would be able to. She picked up the dreamcatcher and held it in her hands; looking at it she saw movement from the corner of her eye and she knew the front door had opened. She took a deep breath and looked up. For the first time in almost a year, there he was, standing in front of her looking every bit as amazing as she remembered. She swallowed hard, cleared her throat and opened the truck door. She felt like she wanted to hide her belly, but knew that was impossible so instead, she lingered with the door open for a moment before slowly closing it. She glanced up at him and saw that look of pain she had seen on his face far more times that she wished she had. She held onto the dream catcher tightly as she walked the few steps to the porch.

"Hi," she said, almost shyly.

"I see you got the gift okay," he said, nodding toward her hands carrying the dreamcatcher.

"It's beautiful..." she paused. "I knew it was you. I'm sorry I came, I just...I knew it was you and I..." She paused as if she needed to catch her breath before speaking again. "I knew you would be here and I needed to say thank you. And to see you." Her voice shook, afraid of this moment because there wasn't any way in which this ended well.

He smiled, although she knew it was hiding his pain. "You look really good."

"I look like a house, but thank you," she said, feeling that old familiar banter with him just begging to come to the surface. "How did you know? About the baby."

"I saw you in town a couple of weeks ago. You were coming out of the drug store." He cleared his throat. "You were with him...and you were laughing. Damn near killed me, but I was glad to see you happy."

Unsure of how to react, she asked, "Do you still come here often?" hoping to change the subject.

"Actually, I'm living here now. At least for the time being. Have been a few months now."

"Living here? Why? Is Amy..."

"No, she's not here. She's...well, she kept the house."

"Kept the house?" Suddenly Hailey felt weak. "You left her." She didn't question it, but said it matter of fact, like she knew he was the one that left and not the other way around.

He nodded.

Suddenly the realization that he might be dating someone else set in and she felt her skin go hot. "Are you seeing someone?" Knowing that if he said yes, she might very well just throw up right then and there.

"No. No, I think I'm past that. I can't uh..." he paused. "I can't see that happening," he finally said.

Although she was relieved, she couldn't help but feel like she had ruined his life. Here she was having a baby with her husband who she loved, staring at a man who she also loved, hearing him tell her he was alone, probably always would be and she was the reason for his pain. She started to panic. "I'm so sorry, I shouldn't have come. I shouldn't have." Walking backward a few steps and then covering her mouth with her hand, her eyes began to well up with tears and she turned away from him. She walked back to her truck as quickly as she could manage, she opened the truck door and paused before getting in. Looking back at him, still standing on the porch, she said "I'm sorry," one last time before getting in and driving away.

The rain had started again as Hailey drove and she couldn't help but feel like it was pretty fitting for her mood and all of the trauma she felt she had caused. She hated that she had hurt Jamie so badly and wished that she had known better than to go see him. For all she knew, that dream catcher was his way of closing the door and she just waltzed right up and opened it all up again, for both of them. She was coming up on the turn for her road when she decided she couldn't bear going home. She blew past it and hit the main road towards town. She didn't know where she was going or why, she just couldn't sit alone in a home filled with memories of her and any man. She needed to be as alone as she could be.

That decision to keep driving was the last thing Hailey remembered when she woke up to lights flashing and people yelling. She couldn't make out what they were saying but through a haze, she knew they were trying to get her attention.

"MISS," she finally made out. A man's voice. "Miss, are you with me?"

She tried to speak but nothing more than a groan came out.

"She's awake!" he yelled. "Keep breathing for me Miss, we're going to get you out of here."

Out of where she wondered? What was happening? Then slowly, things started to come back to her. She had been driving and the rain was picking up. She was in her truck and these people, who were these people? Paramedics. She was hurt. Thoughts rushed through her mind at a million miles an hour.

"My baby" she mumbled.

The sound of metal being torn apart filled the air and Hailey began to panic. Her heart was pounding in her chest and she started to hyperventilate. Her words weren't coming out clearly and she knew they weren't understanding anything she was trying to say.

"One...two...and three," and on that last count, they pulled her from the truck. Pain ripping through her body as they moved her, she knew she wasn't okay.

"MY BABY" she finally cried out before losing consciousness.

Jamie had stood on the front porch for what felt like an eternity after Hailey left. He kept waiting for her to come back, the same way he did the day she told him Will wanted to have a baby with her. He had no idea what he would say if she did come back, but he knew he wished she would. When he realized she was long gone, he turned and walked back inside. An overwhelming sense of loneliness sunk in; he felt like he somehow had lost her for a second time. Sitting here by himself wasn't an option since all he did there on a good day was rerun memories of them together along with every moment she spent in that cabin. Looking around the room he could picture her as clear as if she was really there, laying with him in the bed, curled up on the floor in front of the fireplace in his arms; he couldn't be here. He grabbed his keys and locked the door behind him. Jumping in the truck and headed out to the one place he could find some peace. He had put Joe at a boarding barn just outside of town until he could get the time to put in some proper fencing and a barn at the cabin and decided the weather was rough enough to mean a quiet moment with his horse where no one would bug him. The rain was picking up pretty good but that didn't bother him too much. In fact he welcomed it. He was nearing the barn when he turned onto the main road and saw lights flashing up ahead. He slowed down, realizing there had been some kind of accident. With a few police cars and a tow truck blocking the way, he slowed to a stop to wait for them to let him through. Looking around at the mess, he realized he was seeing two trucks in the ditch, both in pretty bad shape and like a kick in the gut he realized he knew the one that looked like it had been cut in two. Putting his truck in park, he jumped out leaving the driver's door hanging wide open and ran to the side of the road.

"Where is she?!" he demanded. "Is she okay?" He didn't even know who he was asking, he just needed someone to answer.

"Hey, you need to get back in your truck sir," a police officer said as he tried to usher Jamie back from the wreckage.

"Is she in there?" panic ripping him apart as he pushed the officer out of his way and ran down to the truck and looked inside. "The woman that was driving that truck..." He turned back to face the officer. "IS SHE ALIVE?" He screamed the words, begging with everything he had in him that he hadn't lost her.

"She's on route to the hospital in the city. Who are you?"

How was he supposed to answer that question?

"She's alive?!" He yelled again, this time needing the words repeated so he knew they were real.

The police officer looked at him with fear, realizing that this man standing in front of him would do anything to save the woman that came out of that truck. Even if it meant tearing into a police officer to get to her.

"She was when she left here. She was in bad shape though," he finally said. His look said he was sorry and Jamie took from it that she was alive when she left, but wouldn't be for much longer.

Glancing back into the truck, he saw the dream catcher laying on the crumpled floor. He ran over, reached in and picked it up.

"Sir," The officer walked a few steps closer. "Sir...You need to leave. I would suggest you get back in your truck."

Jamie hadn't bothered to listen to the last thing the officer said. He was back in his truck before the officer could even finish talking. He turned around to take a road that wasn't blocked. He needed to get to the hospital and see her even though he knew Will would be there. It didn't matter, if she died, nothing mattered. He was running on instinct.

Will was in the middle of teaching when his phone began to buzz in his pocket. Ignoring it the first time, he continued teaching. When it went off a second time in under a minute, he apologized to the class, making a joke about how it was probably his wife with a weird pregnancy craving.
"Hello?" he said, still with a smile on his face.
"Mr. Jenkins?" said the voice on the other end.
"Yes, speaking."
"Mr. Jenkins, I'm afraid your wife has been in an accident and has been brought into emergency."
Everything stopped. All sounds stopped, all movement stopped. It was as if someone had frozen time.
"Mr. Jenkins, can you hear me?" the voice asked.
"I'm on my way," were the only words Will could muster. He left his notes, his briefcase, even his students. He didn't say a word as he rushed out of the class.

Jamie parked his truck and ran into the emergency room without a second thought, scanning the room trying to get his bearings, he saw the front desk about 40 feet to the left, past a sea of people with random injuries waiting to be seen by a Doctor. But before he could put one foot in front of the other, he realized he was looking at Will, standing at the front desk begging the nurse behind the counter to give him information on his wife. In that moment he knew he needed to keep their secret. It wouldn't do her any good, or god forbid her memory, if this was as bad as he feared, to let Will find out what had happened between the two of them.

Will stepped back from the desk, running his hands through his hair and began to pace.

Jamie didn't want to leave. He couldn't bare the thought of not being there if the worst happened so he found an empty seat in the crowded waiting room and sat down. He picked up a magazine and although he had zero intention of reading it, opened it up and leaned forward, resting his elbows on his knees, magazine in hand hoping his baseball cap would cover his face enough to go unnoticed.

An hour had gone by and Will had spent the entire time pacing. He hadn't seen Jamie sitting there and Jamie hoped that even if he did, he wouldn't have really recognized him anyway. Finally a doctor came out and called Wills name. It got both men's attention and it was everything Jamie could do not to stand up to hear the news first hand. Will began to walk towards the doctor and it was clear that he was going to be led from the waiting room.

"Is she okay? The baby?" Will asked as he approached the large doors and the doctor waiting at the entrance.

Jamie held his breath hoping to have enough time to hear the answer before they disappeared through the doors.

"Mr. Jenkins your wife suffered a great deal of trauma and she's going to need surgery but she should pull through."

Jamie put the magazine down and sat back in his chair, letting out a quite "thank god."

Will and the doctor walked through the emergency room doors and disappeared from Jamie's sight. He sat staring at the floor for fifteen minutes before finally deciding to get up and leave. There wasn't anything he could do for her here and he knew no one would tell him anything about her condition if he asked. He headed for the truck and once inside, picked up the dream catcher and held it the whole drive home.

"Mr. Jenkins, I'm afraid there was simply too much damage caused from the impact that the baby..."

Will's heart sank as he realized what the doctor was saying. Their baby didn't make it and just like when he got the call about the accident, all sounds seemed to stop and he was alone in complete silence.

Nineteen

What's Right Is Wrong

A week had gone by since the accident and although Hailey was alive, she felt like every part of her had died. She was tormented over the loss of her unborn baby and guilty at the thought that she had never fully allowed herself to be truly committed to the family she was building. She had said goodbye to Jamie but there was always a small part of him in every thought she had. Knowing that she had been coming from seeing him when she got in the accident tortured her. Had she just stayed home that day, she would still be pregnant. Her baby would still be alive. Once again, she felt plagued by her wrong choices and was lost in her own guilt.

Jamie had gone to the hospital every day since the accident, but had never let her know he was there. He found out what room she was in and would come close, but never went in. Will had always been in the room with her, at least until today. When he turned the corner toward her room he saw her laying in the hospital bed, looking out the window and all alone. Now it was his turn to know better, but like her, he couldn't help himself. He walked slowly toward her room and paused a step away from the door and just looked at her. Hearing that she would live the day of the accident just wasn't enough, he had to see her, to see her moving and breathing. He needed to hear her voice. Bruises covered her face and arms and he knew that what he was able to see was the least of the damage. He took another step and knocked lightly against the open door.

Hailey looked toward the sound of the knock and let out a quiet sigh at the sight of him. "I wondered if I might see you here."

Jamie walked a few more steps inside the room toward her but stayed standing instead of sitting in the chair beside her bed.

"I've been here every day. I just didn't...well, Will was here each time so I left. I was here when you were brought in. I drove past the accident and when I saw it was your truck..." his voice cracked as he held back tears. "They told me you were on your way here so I came as fast as I could."

"I lost the baby," she said, the tears building in her eyes. Her body felt weak at the thought. "They said the guy that hit me was just distracted. Not paying attention.”

He wanted to touch her, to hold her and make every pain she felt disappear. It was instinct to protect her and comfort her but he couldn't risk getting caught being that close to her. Nor did he know if she would even let him.

“You don’t have to say anything. Everyone’s been trying to say something.” The tone of her voice was dark and frightened. “Nothing really helps, so it's okay to not say anything.”

He knew she was right and so he stood there, never taking his eyes off of her, even as she turned her gaze back to the window.

“I shouldn’t stay, in case Will comes back.”

“I sent him home and told him not to come back until tomorrow,” she said, still looking out the window. “I just needed a break. He means well and I know he’s hurt too, I just...I just needed to not be with him for a little while. I’m just not able to take care of him by being something for him to fix.” Finally she looked back at Jamie, knowing that he was probably the only person she could have said that to without worrying they thought badly of her for saying it.

Feeling like her honesty was an invitation to stay a little longer, Jamie sat down in the chair next to her. “I would have brought flowers but...”

“You don’t need to do that. I’m glad you came though.” She paused to catch her breath and brace herself for what she realized she was about to say. “I didn’t like how I left the cabin. I shouldn’t have gone in the first place, but I shouldn’t have just left like that once I was there. I panicked because I felt horrible for all the pain I've caused you. I've hurt you so badly and I'm so, so sorry."

"You haven't caused me any pain," he said, reaching out and taking her hand. It had been nearly a year since he had touched her last and they both noticed how intense it made them feel. "I'm the one that woke up and realized what I wanted and what I didn't. It wasn't fair to her or me if I had stayed. It just wasn't meant to be. That's not your fault."

"How come you didn't tell me?"

"It wouldn't have been fair to you. You deserve to be happy Hailey. Of course I wanted to, but ..."

"But I had chosen him."

As she said it, she saw the pain in his eyes and knew it was the truth. He hadn't left her that day in the woods. He hadn't pushed her away or been the one to end things. She had left him, he simply just let her go. Had she been there to tell him she was leaving Will because she simply couldn't bring herself to have a family with him and leave Jamie, he would have left his wife and they would have been together. She had spent the last year trying to push her love for him away into the deepest, most tucked away place in her being and here she was, right back at the beginning.

"Hailey, we're going to take you down for your scans now," a nurse said as she leaned in through the door. Jamie's hand slipped from Hailey's and he stood up, preparing himself to leave.

"If it's okay, can you just let me know when you are home, safe?" he asked. "I won't bug you again, I just...I just want to know you are settled and ok," he said as he backed up toward the door.

The look of pain and loss on his face was more than she could handle and she knew that if she spoke, tears would come with the words. She gently nodded yes and he turned and walked away. Her heart felt like it was shattering in a million pieces all over again.

Hailey was discharged from the hospital a few days after Jamie's visit. Will thought bringing her home would help to brighten her spirits, but in reality it made her feel very lost. The sight of the baby's room was harder to process than she imagined and she was still in a great amount of physical pain from her accident but it was her relationship with Will that made it all worse. She was grieving so many losses all at once and there was only one person in the whole world that she could talk to about all of it. That person should have been Will, but it wasn't. The day after she got home, she texted Jamie like he had asked her to.

"I'm home and I'm okay. At least I will be."

She had typed about ten different versions of that text and deleted them all before sending the one that said the least. How could she sit there and tell him how much she loved seeing him if she wasn't with him. How could she tell him she missed him without breaking his heart again? So she erased every word that meant something and simply sent him the text he asked for. 'Let me know when you are home and that you are okay,' he had said.

She didn't hear back from him and truthfully, she hadn't expected to. At some point, he was going to have to forget about her, or at least try to and she knew she had to be willing to let him do that.

Winter had come and gone and although the bruises had disappeared and the cuts had healed, Hailey still struggled. She was just different than she was before the accident and it wasn't something she could hide from Will. He had gone back to working long hours and she had gone back to her routine of writing and spending time in the barn with Charlie. When they were in the house together, they sort of found themselves just going through the motions. At first they had been fighting, mostly because Will was trying to help and even though she knew it was horrible of her, she simply just didn't want him to help her. He wasn't doing anything wrong at all and she tried to bite her tongue but with each passing day, she seemed to realize, without being able to admit it, that it was simply that he was just the wrong person doing the right things.

It was Saturday morning and Hailey had been lying awake for what felt like hours. When the sun came up, she got up quietly, hoping not to wake Will. She headed to the washroom and then to the kitchen to make coffee. By the time she was pouring a cup for herself, she heard Will coming down the hallway.

"Couldn't sleep again?" he asked as he reached for a mug in the cupboard.

"Nope," she said plainly. "You?"

"No."

She stepped aside and let him have room to make a coffee. This had become more or less their routine for the last ten months and they both knew it spoke volumes.

Hailey wrapped her hands around the warm mug of coffee and walked to the windows overlooking the field. Will had walked around the side of the kitchen island and sat down on one of the tall bar stools they had.

"You're wearing your own pyjamas," he said like he was in shock. Hailey turned around to see the look of confusion on his face.

"You've been wearing your own pyjamas since you came home from the hospital. You always used to wear my tee shirts to bed. You've stopped."

Hailey looked down at her clothes. She didn't have an answer to what was obviously a question. She looked back up at him, her mouth parting as if she was about to speak, but no words actually came. She just sort of shrugged her shoulders lightly and shook her head as if to say "I just don't know".

"You're done aren't you?" he asked. His tone was sobering.

She looked into his eyes and knew he was right.

"Will..." she said his name and then paused.

He stood up and put his mug down on the island next to him. His eyes were wide with fear at hearing her answer.

"Will, I don't know...I don't know how to answer that. Are you?"

"Hails, we're going in circles here," he said as the look of fear changed to a look of giving in.

"Will, I love you so much. I always have." She began to smile at the thought.

"I know. I love you too. But it's not enough is it?"

Tears began rolling down her cheeks but they were tears of relief, not of pain. In that moment, she realized that if she really did love Will, she had to let him go. He deserved to be happy and live a life he wanted, not the life he thought she wanted. When they had met, they were wanting the same things and somewhere along the line, she had the chance to grow up and find herself.

Something he had already had the chance to do before her. He had been trying to come along for the ride, but at the end of the day, they weren't creating a life together, one was always going to have to be sacrificing something for the other.

Will walked toward her and wiped the tears from her face before leaning in and kissing her mouth. It was a different kiss than any they had shared before. It was a goodbye, a release and a promise to always love each other.

"I want you to be happy," he said, holding her face in his hands. "And you aren't happy. Neither of us are."

Will took the first few days of the week off and they spent the time together, packing up his things. It just made sense that Hailey kept the farm and Will would find a place in the city where he worked. The three days it took to pack were the first days in a long time that they had just spent actually enjoying each other's company. They laughed and talked like they did when they first met, only making them realize that in the end, they were making the right decision. On Wednesday afternoon, Will's coworker Mike pulled up in a U-Haul truck. Hailey decided to give them some space to load everything so she headed out to the barn to do chores and get some extra things done that had been building up on her to do list. It had been almost two hours before she heard Will come in.

"So, I guess this is it Hails," he said, stopping a few steps away from her.

"I guess so," she said. She shook her head, trying to fight off the tears and said "Come here" as she gestured with her arms for him to come hug her.

"Will, this doesn't mean I don't love you."

"I know. You know I feel the same way. It just wasn't meant to be I suppose."

And with that, he kissed her cheek and walked out of the barn and got in his car. Hailey walked to the barn door and watched him drive away. She wiped the tears from her eyes as they fell and she whispered "goodbye."

Twenty

Every time I See You

Hailey walked into the house and looked around. It was half empty and quiet, aside from the dogs walking in behind her. She was holding tight onto her phone, rubbing her thumb against the back of it like she was trying to put something off. She knew what it was and laughed out loud at the thought.

"What am I doing!?" A mix of fear and excitement washed over her. With no one to answer to but herself, she realized she had been trying to be polite about waiting, but who was she trying to be polite to!? No one was there.

She quickly opened her phone and pulled up Jamie's number to call him. The phone rang five times before going to voicemail. "Dammit," she whispered. He was working and probably wouldn't check his voicemail.

"Text it is," she said to herself.

"Are you free? I know we haven't spoken in a while, but I need to see you, it's really important."

She waited on edge for what felt like an eternity. Even though she knew he wasn't always easy to get a hold of quickly since he couldn't exactly answer his phone in the middle of putting shoes on a horse, she couldn't keep her mind from wandering to the possibility that the longer it took for him to write back, the more it might mean he wasn't writing her back on purpose, trying to avoid getting back into the same situation they had been in before. After all, he had no idea she and Will had ended things and although it might make it easier to get her point across, it wasn't exactly something she wanted to tell him in a text.

She paced the kitchen for ten minutes before she finally decided to distract herself with tidying up. She rearranged the books that were left on the shelf, moving knickknacks here and there, trying to make the things she had left look more like a home.

An hour had passed and Hailey was beginning to get genuinely nervous that she hadn't heard from him yet. She picked up her phone, double checking that the volume was up and that she hadn't missed anything. Nothing. She put it back down and began to busy herself in the kitchen. No sooner had she made it to the sink of dirty dishes, than her phone buzzed. She ran back to where she had left it on the island, nearly dropping it on the floor in her fury to check the message.

After a year and a half apart, he would still drop everything and come for her if she needed him. She felt a sudden rush of heat go through her body and her heart began beating quickly. She felt nervous like a teenager falling in love for the first time.

 She couldn't wipe the smile off her face.

She looked at the time, four o'clock. She had just around two hours until he was there and she needed to shower and make herself look presentable. She went into the bathroom and turned on the shower to let the water warm up while she undressed. As she did, she caught a glimpse of herself in the mirror and was caught off guard. She stopped and stared at her reflection realizing that the reason she looked so different was because she was happy. It was the first time in a very long time that she could say she was truly happy.

She jumped in the shower, washed up and shaved every shaveable area she had, thinking to herself that she should be prepared for anything tonight. Or at least hoping she would need to be. Grabbing a towel, she turned the water off and wrapped herself up before heading down the hall to her room. As she passed what was meant to be the baby's room, she stopped and opened the door. She found herself putting her hands on her belly as if the baby were still there and she stepped inside the empty room. They had returned all the furniture and boxed up all the baby clothes and toys and put them in storage. Her baby would have been born by now, had she not been in the accident and until this very moment Hailey had not been able to feel any happiness in this room. This time, something was different. There was hope here now and instead of focusing on what happened, she found herself thinking of how happy she had been to feel those first little flutters and kicks. She smiled and whispered "I will always love you" before backing out of the room. This time, she left the door open.

Digging through her closet she grabbed the pair of jeans she had worn the day she and Jamie had gone on the trail ride when she got hurt. Sliding them on, she couldn't help but remember how nervous she was putting them on back then and how she couldn't believe she was trying to get his attention. Funny thing was, she was just as nervous this time. She grabbed a plain white tee shirt and pulled it on before heading to the mirror to fix her hair and put on some make up. By the time she was dressed and ready she had about an hour left. Looking around her room, not knowing whether Jamie would even be in here, she grabbed a fresh set of sheets and an extra pillow and made the bed. There was something very unnerving about sharing a bed with him that she had shared with Will but changing the sheets would have to do for now.

She headed back into the kitchen and washed up the couple of dishes that were in the sink before deciding that although she had almost no time left to make this anymore special, she wanted to try. She grabbed all of the candles that she had laying around and placed them on the kitchen table, island and coffee table. She dimmed

the lights in the living room and found a lighter to light
the candles. It was only April and the evenings still had
a chill to them so she built a small fire in the living room
fireplace. With the flames giving off a romantic glow she
felt like she was ready. It wasn't until her phone buzzed
again that she felt her heart start to race.

*"Heading your way now. Should be there in twenty
minutes."*

What if he had moved on? She knew he had told
her he didn't ever see that happening, but time changes
things and he wasn't exactly an unattractive guy. It's not
like he didn't have options or women interested in him
pretty much constantly.

"Get it together Hailey," she scolded herself. She
stood by the front door going back and forth about how
she wanted to handle this and what she should say first.
The longer she stood there, the more nervous she got.

"This is insane!" she said to herself and decided to
go for a shot of liquid courage. She headed to the fridge
and grabbed a cheap bottle of rosé, opened it up and took
a couple of huge swigs of it. Not exactly the classiest
thing she could recall doing, but she hoped it would help.
She tossed the bottle back in the fridge and went back to
waiting at the door. Before too long she heard his truck
coming up the laneway. It was a sound she had grown to
know by heart and had spent what must add up to hours
waiting for it during the time they were together. Her
back straightened and she took a deep breath as his truck
came into view. Parking in front of the house, he turned
the truck off and stepped out cautiously. He looked
toward the barn first, before glancing back at the sound of
the screen door opening at the house. Hailey stepped out
onto the porch but she couldn't say a word. The sight of

him took her breath away and she realized it was the first time she had laid eyes on him when she was actually allowed to feel what she was feeling for him.

"Hey," he said, still clearly a little confused about what was going on.

"Hey," she said back with a smile.

"Is everything okay?"

She nodded yes. "I know, this is weird. We haven't really seen each other or spoken in almost two years and I ask you to come here out of the blue..." her voice began to trail off and almost under her breath but still loud enough for him to hear, she said "...and now saying that I realize I might be making a complete fool of myself."

"Hailey," he said. He had a way of snapping her back into reality when she started to freeze up.

"Come inside." She turned and walked back into the house, letting the screen door swing shut behind her.

Jamie walked up the porch steps, grabbed the door handle and as he opened it to walk inside he felt his breath catch in his chest. There she was, surrounded by candlelight looking as beautiful as he had ever seen her.

He walked through the kitchen and stopped a few feet before her.

"Hailey, what's going on?"

She took a deep breath in. Knowing that the only way to start this conversation was to just let it spill out of her.

"Jamie, I fell in love with you the moment I met you. The time we spent together was the only time in my whole life where I felt truly myself and felt so perfectly connected to another soul. I have spent the last year and a half trying to force myself to live without you and to pretend that we could both be happy living apart but all I was succeeding in doing was causing myself and everyone around me to be miserable. Jamie, I'm in love with you! I want all of you and everything with you." Her nervous smile had turned into a look of pure need.

Jamie stood there, clearly running a million things through his mind at once. "What about Will? What about starting a family with him? Where is he?"

"He left early this afternoon." She paused. "And he's not coming back." As the words came from her mouth, she let out a sigh of relief. She shrugged her shoulders, as if to admit this had always been the right choice all along. "Jamie, I'm yours, all of me, forever…if you still want me."

No sooner had the words fallen off her lips than he was across the room, pulling her into him and kissing her with more passion than either of them had ever thought possible. When they broke free of their kiss, he lifted her up off her feet and looking into her eyes he said "Of course I still want you. I want nothing but you."

They didn't make it to the bedroom, instead, they melted into each other right there on the living room floor, surrounded by candle light. Each touch felt like the first time they were discovering each other that day at the cabin. Even though it wasn't new, and they both had each other's bodies memorized at this point, the fact that they were both finally free to choose this made it feel new again.

Afterwards, Jamie reached up and grabbed the blanket off the couch and a couple of throw pillows. They curled up together and just took each other in. Knowing that neither had to run off before they got caught or get back to work so it didn't look like they were sneaking around. Neither of them wanted to talk about what happened with Will and why he was gone. That was a conversation for another time. Tonight, it was just about them. As they laid together in each others arms, Jamie placed his hand on Hailey's stomach and began to trace his fingers over her scar from the accident. Normally, she was very timid to even touch it herself, but for some reason she felt a comfort as his skin brushed against it, as if he were somehow able to take the pain away.

"I don't know what I would have done if..." he couldn't finish the sentence. "When I saw it was your truck in the ditch, I lost it. I just needed you to be okay."

"I don't remember the accident, just waking up after it happened. You were the last thing I remember. Loving you and just feeling broken because I couldn't be with you. I am so sorry for everything. I caused you so much pain because I just didn't know what I was doing. I was trying to do the right thing. I was...I just made a mess of everything instead."

They laid in silence for a moment almost as if allowing the past pain to wash away with each minute that went by. As his hand came to rest on her stomach Hailey put her hand over his.

"You know, I used to daydream that the baby was yours. I'd hold my hand on my belly and try with everything I had in me to imagine your hand was underneath mine, just like this."

"I'll be right back," Jamie said as he jumped up, grabbed his jeans and slipped them on. Hailey sat up, pulling the blankets up to cover herself, wondering what had caused him to get up like that in the middle of what she thought was a pretty intense conversation.

Jamie headed out to his truck in the dark, returning a minute later with what looked like a folded up

tea towel. He sat back down next to Hailey and held it out
to her.

"I took it from your truck when I saw the accident.
Damn near got arrested for doing it too."

As she looked into his eyes, she realized what he
had handed her. Unwrapping it from the towel, tears
began to fall from her eyes.

"I didn't know what happened to it. I thought it
had been destroyed or lost," she said, reaching up and
wrapping her arms around his neck.

He pulled her up onto his lap, her legs wrapped
around his waist and he wiped the tears from her eyes.

"Move in with me," she said. "Bring Joe and come
live with me and Charlie. Wake up next to me every
morning. I want to spend the rest of my life with you
Jamie Sutton."

"On one condition...make that two," he said with a
smile, letting his hands slide down her arms and onto her
waist.

"One?" she asked

"Marry me?"

She gave him a coy look, trying to hold back her
smile as if she actually had to consider her answer. "And
two?"

"Have babies with me?"

A sudden flash to the conversation in the woods
where he told her that had they met at a different time,
he'd be the one asking her to have a baby came flooding
into her mind. She reached up and put her hands on
either side of his face, feeling the slight roughness of his
beard starting to poke through.

"Yes," she said, leaning in to kiss him, but just
before their lips met, she paused, holding herself almost

close enough for their lips to touch and just before
allowing herself to completely and utterly fall into him,
she whispered "...And yes."

Author Biography

Claire Whitmore grew up in a small town in Ontario, Canada where she fell in love with nature and subsequently found her happy place. A day dreamer from the get go, Claire knew from an early age that storytelling was her calling, often wandering into the woods with a notebook and pencil to spend the day lost in whatever world her imagination would create.

Claire, who still resides in Ontario, lives with her husband and two children who share in her love of the outdoors. When not letting her imagination run away with a new story, she can be found riding the trails or spending time in the barn with her horses.